DATE DUE

MURDER

Unscripted

MURDER

Unscripted

A HOLLYWOOD MYSTERY

Clive Rosengren

PERFECT CRIME BOOKS

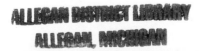

Printed in the United States of America.

Perfect Crime Books™ is a registered Trademark.

Cover Photo: Copyright © 2012 BigStock. Used by permission.
Author Photo: Larry Rosengren.

This book is a work of fiction. The characters, entities and institutions are products of the Author's imagination and do not refer to actual persons, entities, or institutions.

Library of Congress Cataloging-in-Publication Data
Rosengren, Clive
Murder Unscripted / Clive Rosengren
ISBN: 978-1-935797-19-7

First Edition: February 2012

For the members of Monday Mayhem.
Thanks for your help in bringing
this story to fruition.

MURDER
Unscripted

Prologue

Lance Grimsley didn't think he could continue this much longer. It wasn't because the woman wasn't a good kisser. In fact, the lip-lock Ruby Landreaux had on him right now was world class, her tongue darting to places even his orthodontist didn't know he had.

And it wasn't because of the environment. The fire was roaring. The snow was blowing outside the cabin. The bearskin rug felt like he'd always thought a bearskin rug should feel. A polar bear to boot.

But it was the damn eyelash. The upper rim of her right eyelash had come loose from its mooring and looked like a spider waiting for a fly.

Ruby reeled in her tongue and released him. "Oh, God, Lance, I didn't think it could be this good," she panted, as she fell back onto the bearskin. Lance propped himself up on one elbow and gazed down at her. A smile tugged at his mouth as he looked at the spider over her right eye.

"I didn't either," he forced himself to say. "We should have been doing this for months."

"We will from now on, darling," Ruby breathed. She ran her fingers through his wavy blond hair, grabbed him by the neck and planted another lip-lock on him.

The wind whistled outside the mountain cabin, kicking up small puffs of snow in the corners of the windows. The kiss continued, chins and lips moving and grinding. Finally, the lovers broke apart and Lance flopped onto his back, sighing and looking up at the raw wooden beams of the ceiling.

Now Ruby propped herself up on an elbow and looked down at him. Not to be outdone, the eyelash over her left eye also started to exhibit characteristics of an arachnid.

"Do you think you can get the divorce?" Ruby asked.

"I don't know. Marsha can be a difficult bitch sometimes."

"You have to talk to her, Lance. I can't go on like this. These weekends take forever to get here and then all of a sudden they're gone in a truffle."

That was it. Two spiders, then a "truffle." Lance burst into laughter, and Ruby sat up, the heavy blanket falling from her shoulders to reveal pasties on each of her ample breasts.

"What the hell's the matter?"

"I'm sorry, I—" Lance stifled another laugh. "The eyelashes, I-I can't—" He doubled over in laughter as Ruby reached for a small compact mirror next to her. She looked at herself, saw the crawling spiders, then stood up, displaying a voluptuous body adorned with only the pasties and the briefest of bikinis.

She glanced to her left where a clump of people hovered over a video monitor, the vastness of a huge sound stage looming behind them. Ruby hurled the mirror to the floor and began marching toward the knot of people, Lance's laughter continuing behind her.

Dean Snider pulled a pair of headphones from his ears and stood up. "Cut it," he yelled.

The fire went out, the wind stopped, and a loud buzzer sounded. Stage 7 on the Americana Pictures lot came to a grinding halt. Again. Low moans rumbled around the cavernous room. A few crew members stalked toward the craft services tables, muttering to one another and shaking their heads in disgust.

Ruby Landreaux was actually Elaine Weddington, and she was mad. Mad as hell. Snider extended a placating hand as she approached him.

"This is really getting to be a royal pain in the ass!" Elaine roared. She swatted aside a robe offered her by a wardrobe assistant. Elaine Weddington almost in her birthday suit was nothing new on the set of *Flames of Desire*.

"Elaine, I'm sorry," Snider pleaded. "We'll go again. The take was no good. We had a boom problem."

"Boom problem? You've got an actor problem," Elaine replied. She snatched from Snider's hands the discarded robe, which he had picked up and was handing her as a peace offering. She slung the flimsy robe around her shoulders, which really didn't accomplish much in the way of covering the anchors of the pasties.

Lance Grimsley, whose real name was Josh Bauer, trotted up to the film's star, a blanket draped around his lean midriff. Elaine whipped around to face him.

"And you, you putz!"

"I'm sorry, Elaine, I couldn't help it," Josh said, his voice quivering in fright. "The damn rug was tickling, truffle, and the eyelash—"

Elaine advanced on the young man, jabbing her finger in his face. "Not only are you a lousy goddamn actor, but you insist on blocking me from the lens whenever there's a clinch. And your kisses taste like pickled pigs' feet."

Josh backed away from her and tripped over a large electrical cable. He lost his grasp on the blanket around his midriff. It fell to the floor, followed by Elaine's glare. Once again, she pointed. "That's nothing to write home about either."

With a toss of her raven mane, she started to stomp off the set, Dean Snider in tow, begging, "Elaine, give me two minutes to fix the shot and we'll go again."

"Like hell we will. I've had it!" She stopped and whirled on the film's diminutive director. "For days now I've been telling you this ear infection is driving me nuts. I'm sick, and I'm pissed off. When you tell me you've hired an actor who can stay in the goddamn scene, then I'll tell you when we'll go again."

Robe trailing behind her, she stormed toward the sound stage door. A bearded technician looked at her, grinned, and nodded his head in approval of her twin peaks as she stomped by him. She stopped in mid-stride. "Enjoying the show, asshole?" She followed with a roundhouse slap to the man's face, sending him reeling against a light stand, knocking both it and him to the floor.

Before he could get to his feet, Elaine Weddington had disappeared through the door, leaving silence in her wake. Several of the crew turned and looked at each other in awe, realizing that they had just witnessed what may have been one of Elaine's finest performances.

The silence was shattered by Snider's clipboard hitting the concrete floor. He kicked it into the cameraman's shin and stood seething. Betty Murphy, his first assistant director, sidled up to him. The picture was a week behind schedule and in danger of going slightly over-budget, which was unheard of at Americana.

"Should I break everyone for lunch?" Betty asked.

"Yeah, what the hell else can I do?" Snider looked at his watch and shook his head. "Give Her Highness an hour and let's see what happens. Maybe she'll cool off."

"All right, everyone, that's lunch. One hour," Betty called.

The rest of the stage lights came on and the crew started to leave through the huge doors.

Josh Bauer walked up to Snider, nervously clasping the blanket around him. "Dean, I'm sorry, man, but I lost it. She had the wrong line, truffle for trifle, and the eyelashes, I—" The mere thought of it made him convulse into laughter again. After a moment, he was joined by both Snider and Betty.

Snider clapped the young actor on the shoulder. "I know, I know, it's not your fault. There's always something with her."

Josh rolled his eyes in relief and took the robe offered by a wardrobe person. "So that scene wasn't unusual?"

"Not really," Snider replied. "And now with this infection, she's twice as bad."

"Come on, Dean, cut her some slack," Betty Murphy said. "It can't be that easy for her when she's hurting." Snider shrugged his shoulders and Josh started for the stage door. "Same setup after lunch?" Betty continued.

"Yeah, we gotta get it today." Snider started to walk off, then turned back. "Did she get her medication?"

"Yes."

"Good. Maybe the bitch will choke on it." When Betty turned to him with a scowl, he put up his hands in defense. "Okay, okay," he said.

An hour later, Leslie Anderson, the second assistant director, left the production trailer and walked the short distance to Elaine Weddington's dressing room, a large mobile home with living quarters protruding outward on hydraulic tracks.

She tapped on the door, opened it and saw Jody Burgess, the star's assistant, at his usual position. Bose headphones covered his ears. They were plugged into an iPod. Jody was doing needlepoint. Leslie watched the muscles ripple under Jody's tee shirt as he made the needle fly through a pattern of lilies in a vase. He finally noticed her and pulled off the headphones.

"Hi," Leslie said. "She eat anything?"

"A yogurt."

"She awake?"

"Dunno." He gestured toward the bedroom. "Be my guest."

Leslie climbed up into the trailer and walked down the hallway to the closed bedroom door. She rapped lightly on it.

"Miss Weddington?"

No reply. She rapped again.

"Miss Weddington? We're ready on the set."

Leslie turned the knob and pushed the door open. Elaine was lying on her left side, her back to the door. Leslie called softly again. She walked around the bed.

Elaine's left hand clenched the pillow. Her right arm hung toward the floor. An overturned bottle of medicine and a dropper lay by a small stain on the carpet.

Leslie gasped in fright. She rushed back to the front of the trailer.

"Jody, have you got a call sheet?" She pulled a cell phone from her belt.

He jerked the headphones from his ears. "What's the matter?"

"Give me the on-set doctor's number!"

Jody fumbled through some paper, thrust a page at her.

"What the hell's the matter?"

"I don't know. It's Elaine."

"Oh, shit." Jody rushed to the bedroom, knelt reached for Weddington's wrist. After a moment he shouted down the hallway. "She hasn't got a pulse!"

Leslie appeared in the doorway and knelt beside Jody. "Doc's on his way."

"Did you call 911?"

"The doctor said he'd do it." Leslie noticed the stain on the floor and reached for the overturned medicine bottle.

"Don't touch anything, Leslie. This might be a crime scene."

"A crime scene? Why?"

Jody reached out and pushed a strand of Elaine's hair off her forehead. "You ever hear of ear drops causing your heart to stop?"

Chapter One

When my phone went off, I was sitting on a fake rock biting into what might have been my fortieth chicken breast, give or take a few. There were also thighs and drumsticks along there somewhere. The cell was in the vibration mode, and when it went off I almost choked. I couldn't look to see who called, but I knew it had to be Mavis, my secretary. She was the only one who had the number.

I was sitting next to Sidney Thornton, who was also on a fake rock. We were perched in front of a fake campfire, dressed like cowboys, shooting a television commercial for Chubby's Chicken and trying to love the hell out of every fake minute of it. It was difficult because our director, Gil Crawford, was acting like Simon Legree without the whip. Apparently he'd won an award a few years back, and ad execs thought he was D. W. Griffith reincarnated.

Of course the days of D. W. Griffith and Cecil B. DeMille with their jodhpurs and jaunty berets are gone. Nowadays an actor is more likely to be directed by intense young men hunched over small video monitors, watching the scene as it's being shot. Gil didn't trust the monitor, or else he didn't trust his director of photography, because we were doing take after take and going through chicken like we owned the ranch.

Sidney wasn't looking too well. Earlier in the day, Penni Wilson, the cute little production assistant with freckles running down the front of her tank-top to places I shouldn't be looking, had asked us if we wanted a spit-bag. I immediately said I did. Sidney declined and looked at me like I was deranged. "Excuse me, Eddie, but what's a spit-bag?"

"We're going to get pretty sick of chicken. Spit it out after each take. You'll see some pretty good residuals from this thing, Sidney. They'll look even better if you can't taste the product."

"Mr. Collins is right, Sidney," Penni chipped in. "You'll lose your taste for it after a while. It'll show in your performance."

I didn't know who Chubby was, or if there even was a Chubby, but I was willing to bet even he couldn't bite into forty chicken breasts, smile into the camera like a

Neanderthal idiot and tell the folks that Chubby's was the best dang chicken to ever come out of an egg.

Penni had given Sidney another chance on the spit-bag, but he still declined. After seventeen takes, he relented. Nevertheless, right now he was looking a little peaked around the beak.

So at the moment the phone went off, Sidney and I were chewing our Chubby's Chicken and looking like we had died and gone to the last roundup in the sky. We held the moment for what seemed to be as long as a David Lean film until Gil shouted "cut!" and Penni came forth with the spit-bags.

I pulled my phone from underneath my chaps, which were so damn old they smelled like they had ridden with Butch and Sundance. Sure enough, it was Mavis at Collins Investigations. She had finally convinced me to get one of these things. If the opportunity to use it came along, she pounced on it like an egg-sucking dog.

Gil gave us five minutes to wash down the chicken while the crew added another light. I headed for the hole in the wall the production company was calling our dressing room. I told myself that a day around Chubby's fire was going to put a few more pennies into the pension fund, so I shouldn't complain. When I came out, Penni was bearing down on me with a frown on her face.

"Mr. Collins, can I talk to you?"

"Yeah, Penni. We ready to go again?"

"Well, actually, we've got a little problem."

I dropped my voice and said, "What? Gil wants a wagon train?" She rolled her eyes and managed a little giggle. I had a hunch Gil wasn't the most popular director the crew had ever worked with.

She said, "Sidney tossed his cookies all over the fake rocks."

"Oh, Christ. Bad Chubby's?"

"I don't think so, but we're going to stop anyway. We need to check your availability for tomorrow."

"Yeah, I'm fine, no problem." Since my agent had been able to wrangle a few bucks more than scale out of them for the session, another day wouldn't hurt.

"Great. I'll tell the producers." She headed for the knot of advertising people sitting in their director's chairs. They all looked very glum, like they had just been informed that Chubby's Chicken had been put on the endangered species list.

Gil walked up to me and stuck out his hand. "Good show, Eddie. Sidney seems to be feeling a bit plungy. We needed to rethink a sticky wicket on the set anyway, so we'll pack it in, get it straightened out, and have another go at it tomorrow, eh?"

I nodded and debated whether to ask him from which Masterpiece Theatre series he'd picked up his accent. However, discretion prevailed. I started untying my stinking leather chaps as I walked back to the hole in the wall. Sidney stood in just his cowboy boots and shorts, draining a glass of water. A credit to the craft.

"You gonna make it, pardner?"

"Oh, Christ, Eddie. I should have followed your advice from the first take. I've never been so sick of chicken in my life."

"Well, get some rest and we'll hit it again tomorrow."

He nodded. The mere thought of more chicken must have been the trigger. He darted into the bathroom. I heard the tell-tale groans of Chubby's Chicken on the rise as I got dressed. I ducked out, signed out with Penni, and headed for the parking lot.

Mavis picked up the office line on the second ring. "Collins Investigations."

"It's your boss, kiddo. What's up?"

"You got a call from a guy by the name of Chad Wentworth. Vandalia Bond and Casualty. You know him?"

"I don't know him, but I've worked with Vandalia. What did he want?"

"Sounds like he's got a job for you. Something to do with Americana Pictures."

She gave me the number and I reached Chad Wentworth. He said, "You've worked for us in the past?"

"A few years back. What's up?"

"We hold the completion bond on a picture called *Flames of Desire*. It's shooting over at Americana. Are you familiar with them?"

"Absolutely. Sam Goldberg's studio."

"Yes. As a matter of fact, he referred you to us. Apparently a death has occurred on the set. There's a good chance the project could be in jeopardy. We'd like to put you on retainer to look into it for us."

"All right," I said, taking my notebook from my pocket.

"Goldberg suggested you come to his office to get up to speed. I've got your previous contract in front of me. Is your fee still the same?"

"Yes, sir."

"Very good. Then until you drop by the office, we'll use our conversation as a handshake. Is that acceptable?"

"Okay by me." I wrote down the address as he gave it to me. "Who died?"

I heard him shuffling some papers. "One of the stars. Elaine Weddington."

My pen froze above the slip of paper as I stared at the phone. After a few long moments, Wentworth called my name.

I put the phone back to my ear. "Yes, yes, I'm here."

"Is there anything else you need from me, Mr. Collins?"

"No, I don't think so."

"Well, then, I'll look forward to meeting with you." He rang off.

I stood in shock. My knees felt like they were going to buckle. A completion bond company insured a movie, protecting a producer's investment in case something should go wrong during the production.

Something had definitely gone wrong on this movie. And it resonated deeply with me.

Elaine Weddington was my ex-wife.

Chapter Two

Fog hovered low over the Hollywood hills, making the famous sign barely visible. Elaine and I had acted like a couple of teenagers when we first saw it together. I had taken her picture up at the Griffith Observatory with the sign in the background. As the wipers of my Cutlass droned back and forth, I felt an old emptiness. Elaine and I hadn't crossed paths in two or three years. When we had, we were glad it happened and spent a few minutes catching up. She was working. I was auditioning. She looked to be in good health. An untimely death like this wasn't supposed to happen.

I headed west. The emptiness grew.

We had met working on an industrial training film. She played my secretary. The dialogue they had given us sounded like it had been written by a nuclear physicist, or the proverbial twelve monkeys. We laughed a lot. It continued when the job was completed.

We discovered we had things in common. We talked movies, argued their merits and failures. We walked the beach trying to define for each other the way we approached the business of acting. Neither of us thought it was difficult. After a few martinis one night, we rousted a Justice of the Peace out of bed and got married.

It wasn't long before Elaine started to get some good visibility in the business. I, on the other hand, came up short too many times. While she started to hit it big, I started to hit the bottle. My boozing came between us, and we split.

Several years passed before I saw her again. By that time, she was starring in a lot of smaller, low-budget films. Many of them weren't good, but she redeemed herself and the films, as much as she could. She had been glad to see me. Sam Goldberg was using her often, and after she arranged for us to meet, Sam put me in several of his pictures. Nothing big. Second cop from the right, that sort of thing. But I needed the work, and he had always seemed to be there.

A few years back, after a long period of being "between engagements," as they say, I got a job as a security guard at a Brentwood gated community. That's when I decided to explore the possibility of getting a PI license. I carried a piece with the security job, and along with three years of working for Uncle Sam as an MP, I had the qualifications to get the license.

After telling me I was a damn fool to quit acting, Sam Goldberg bankrolled me in setting up an office. Now it was my livelihood, with occasional acting jobs when there was time.

A stoplight caught me near the Americana entrance. To my left a billboard announced the arrival of Americana Pictures' production *Island Mistress*, starring names I recognized from somewhere. Probably some long-cancelled television series. Actors trying to keep the dream alive worked cheap, and Sam knew it. The billboard sat atop one of the sound stages on the lot. I pulled in and glided up to the security shed at the front gate.

The guard was Al Butler. He was a short, stocky man with a small moustache. I recognized him from another time I had been on the lot. The recognition wasn't mutual. He said curtly, "Help you?"

"Eddie Collins to see Sam Goldberg."

He checked a clipboard. "I don't have you on my list."

"He's expecting me. Call his office."

Butler phoned the office and wrote me a parking pass. "In the garage to your right. Leave this on the dash."

He wasn't having a good day. I knew how he felt.

Chapter Three

Sam Goldberg wasn't a major player in Hollywood anymore, but he'd been around forever. He started working at Paramount in the fifties as a gofer, hanging around the sound stages, asking questions of anybody about everything before working his way into producing. Along with a few other investors, he founded Americana Pictures in the late sixties.

Nobody knew who those investors were, but Sam spent their money wisely. He made lower-budget pictures that always seemed to find an audience, if not here then overseas or in the home video market. The pictures were short on sophistication but strong on plot. The bad guys were bad, and the good guys made them pay. Sam made an extra buck renting his studio space to independent production companies. You never knew what was shooting on the lot.

This must have been pirate week. I walked around a corner and almost bumped into two buccaneers rattling sabers under the watchful eye of a fight choreographer. The guy with the patch over his right eye seemed to be on the losing end. I watched his moves for a couple of seconds. The patch wasn't his only handicap. His lunges looked more like slips on a banana peel.

The hallway leading to Sam's office smelled of old dust and strong disinfectant. Americana Pictures had been on this piece of real estate for quite a few years now. Before that, the lot had gone through a long list of tenants, some big, some only middling. No doubt some of Hollywood's legends had walked these halls at one time or another. I sure as hell wasn't one of them, but it was a kick to fantasize.

I pushed open the door and saw Thelma Hendricks sitting at her computer, her back to me. Thelma had put up with Sam for as long as I could remember. She kept his schedule in front of him, fended off callers, and generally walked point for him.

Large, old, over-stuffed furniture, no doubt pulled off some film set, filled the room. The two sofas looked like too many nervous starlets had sharpened their fingernails on the arms.

Thelma glanced at a spreadsheet to the right on her desk and caught sight of me. She got to her feet.

"Thelma, you vixen, how the hell are you?" I said, enveloping her in a bear hug. She was probably fifty-something, but kept herself looking good. She always dressed in richly-colored blouses that gave the faint suggestion of a woman who didn't mind staying out late. As she grabbed me, I detected a trace of a perfume that reminded me of orange blossoms. She pulled back and held my face in her hands.

"Oh, God, Eddie, I'm so sorry. The dailies were just terrific. She looked so good." She kissed me on my cheek. "Go right in. Sam's waiting."

Sam's office smelled of cigar smoke. I had never seen Sam Goldberg without a cigar in his mouth and stains of ashes on his clothes. If he ever used an ashtray, it was news to me. The room was empty. I looked around for him, then heard the toilet flush and the sound of running water coming from his private bathroom.

The walls of his office were covered with posters from Sam's movies. I recognized the names of several of them, even one in which I had appeared. Elaine's name highlighted a title called *High Sierra Scandal*. If I remembered correctly, the closest she had ever got to the Sierras was a couple of days in the San Gabriel Mountains above Glendale. She'd brought home a hell of a head cold for that.

Sam came out of the bathroom. He was rotund and had very little hair left on the top of his head. Years ago he had tried wearing a rug, until Thelma told him he looked like a cue ball with moss. He'd thrown away the rug and pouted for a week.

Now he was in shirtsleeves and rumpled trousers. He grabbed me by the shoulders, pulled my head down, and planted a sloppy kiss on my forehead.

"Eddie, m' boy, how the hell are ya?"

"I've been better, Sam."

"Yeah, I know. A hell of a thing, huh?"

He walked over to his liquor cabinet and jerked the glass top out of a decanter of bourbon. "What time is it?"

I slid the cuff away from my Timex special. "Three-thirty."

"You want a belt?"

Sam splashed three fat fingers of whiskey into two tumblers, handed me one. "So, Vandalia got hold of you?"

"Yeah. What happened to Elaine?"

"I don't know for sure. The LAPD—"

"Why are they involved?"

"We don't know. The cops said they might have to rule it a crime scene." He finished off his drink, refilled the glass. "Crissakes, that's all I need."

I stood there stunned. A crime scene?

Sam said, "She apparently had another fight with the director and stomped off the set. They found her an hour later in her trailer."

He jammed a cigar into his mouth and winced. Muttering, he yanked open the center drawer of the desk and pulled out a small bottle. He used the bottle's eyedropper top to squirt something onto a back tooth. His pain seemed to ease. "You're working this for Vandalia, but I want to hear from you. I care what happened to Elaine."

I didn't object, and he punched a button on his intercom. "Thelma, call the production manager on Stage 7. Tell them Eddie is working for my insurance company. He's got complete access to the set."

"Right away," she answered. "Security called. Press vans are at the front gate. They want onto the lot."

"Goddamn vultures. Tell the gate to let them through." Sam looked at me. "I suppose even bad publicity don't hurt."

"Can you finish the picture?" I asked.

"Hell, I don't know. The director says he thinks he can. He says he can use Elaine's double. Shoot her in long shots, over her shoulder, stuff like that. It's going to require script changes and re-shooting. I don't know if my money guys are gonna go for it. Or what the bond guys will decide." He reached over and clapped me on the shoulder. "Had you seen her lately?"

"Two or three years ago."

"You still have feelings for her?"

"You don't live with someone for years and just forget about them."

"Yeah. Listen, Eddie. You and I both know Elaine probably burned some bridges along the way, but she was a great kid. If someone did something to her, I want to know about it."

"You will," I said.

Thelma fixed me up with a security badge and parking pass.

"Thanks," I said. "Can you get me a copy of the screenplay?"

She went over to a shelf and pulled down a bound screenplay. "Who comes up with these titles?"

"Somebody making a lot more money than you and me, Thelma."

Chapter Four

I walked toward Stage 7, paging through *Flames of Desire*. The lot had gotten busy. Dodging a messenger in a golf cart brought me into the company of a herd of extras, or "background," or "atmosphere"—I can't keep up with whatever they're calling them these days. Several sat on lawn chairs with phones to their ears, wearing the intense look of people asking agencies where they would be tomorrow. As I stepped around a pirate and a belly dancer, I saw a familiar face. Nick Nolte, looking better than he had in the infamous booking shot seen round the world, was puffing a cigarette as he ran dialogue with another actor. Nolte and I had exchanged punches in a film a while back. He was making the big bucks, so he won. But I had rung his chimes a couple of times, and he had been impressed enough that on the next take he had put my lights. We had shared a couple of beers afterward. It didn't mean he would recognize me today.

At the end of a huge sound stage I saw the tell-tale yellow of crime scene tape, which surrounded a dressing-room trailer. A black-and-white police unit sat near the trailer's open door, next to an unmarked car and what looked like a forensics van. The van's rear doors were open. A portable table had been set up under an awning. Two small floodlights illuminated several plastic chests on the table.

A cluster of reporters and cameramen crowded in. A uniformed officer stood in front of them, fending off shouted questions.

As I started toward the big door of the sound stage, another cop strutted up and slapped his hand on my shoulder. I looked up and saw a name tag that said Martin. His uniform was starched to the point where I wondered how he sat down.

"The name's Eddie Collins." I showed him the ID tag around my neck. He was underwhelmed. "Sam Goldberg gave me permission to look around."

"Who's Sam Goldberg?"

"He owns the pavement you're standing on."

"I don't care if he's Albert Hitchcock. This is a crime scene and it's off-limits."

I looked at him and noticed the little smirk on his face. He thought he had me. I was tempted to ask him what his favorite Albert Hitchcock movie was, but decided against it.

"Then who's in charge of the crime scene, Officer Martin?"

"Lieutenant Rivers."

"Lieutenant Rivers? Well, would you tell Charlie I'd like to see him?"

Martin looked like he was only holding a pair of deuces and his bluff had been called. He slunk off to a group of crime scene personnel at the door of the sound stage.

I'd known Charlie Rivers for several years. He'd helped me out a time or two when I needed something other than red tape from the LAPD, and we'd become pretty good friends. He came over and stuck out a burly paw. "If it isn't Eddie 'the actor' Collins." He was carrying a can of Diet Pepsi, but otherwise he looked like he'd never met a Philly cheesesteak he didn't love. "You working on the lot?" he asked.

"I am now. Goldberg's insurance company has got me on retainer."

"Why is that?"

"They'll have to pay off if the picture is shut down."

Charlie's eyes narrowed a little. He tilted the Diet Pepsi back, drained it, and made a perfect throw into a nearby trash bin.

"I also knew the deceased. Thought I'd drop around and see if you needed any information about her."

"How did you know her?"

"She was my ex-wife."

"No kiddin'?" He signaled me to follow him into the sound stage.

"What kind of cops are you raising here?" I asked.

"What do you mean?"

"Your Officer Martin thinks *Psycho* was directed by Albert Hitchcock."

"Poor guy. I think he wants to be an actor when he retires."

That wasn't out of the realm of possibility. Retired and off-duty cops worked security on movie locations around town. The chow was good and plentiful. Now and then a cop might get himself into a scene.

In a corner of the sound stage, LAPD had set up a makeshift interrogation area around some folding tables. Detectives were hunched over them, peering into the faces of witnesses, maybe potential suspects. They talked in whispers.

As we walked, Charlie said, "So explain this insurance deal to me."

"The producer has to enter into a completion bond. It insures that the picture will be delivered on time and within budget. If something goes wrong and the picture can't be completed, the insurer wants to know why before they have to pay off the investors."

"And the thing that goes wrong could be a murder?"

"Yes. Is that what you've got here?"

"We're treating it as suspicious. It could be a lot of things, including an accident or an OD."

I felt a wrenching stab of grief. "What happened?"

Charlie looked at me, his eyebrows raised. "I can't share case details with you."

"Come on, she was my ex. Maybe I can help."

"Maybe." He took a notebook from his shirt. "The company broke for lunch about one o'clock. An hour later the victim was found in her trailer with what appeared to be a bottle of medicine on the floor next to her. A prescription for an ear infection."

"Allergic reaction?"

"Do you know if she had allergies?"

"When we were together, she didn't. Was the medicine tainted?"

"Inconclusive at this point, but I wouldn't bet against it. So the two of you were divorced? How long ago?"

"Eight and a half years."

"Were you still in touch?"

"Not really. I ran into her from time to time."

"When's the last time?"

"Almost three years ago."

"Friendly meeting?"

"I'd say so."

"Wish I could say the same thing about my ex. I sometimes think she's got a contract out on me."

"Where you going with this, Charlie?"

"Just trying to get some of this information you talked about. Where were you earlier today?"

"Am I a suspect, Lieutenant?"

"You should know the drill, Eddie."

"I was shooting a commercial for Chubby's Chicken." I reached into the pocket of my trench coat and pulled out the call sheet for the morning shoot. "You'll find the name and address of the production company on the top of the page. The location of the lot is right underneath it."

Charlie looked at the sheet and handed it back to me. He turned as a man and a woman approached. The man was Jim Haggerty, an LAPD detective. He was tall and gaunt, wearing a suit with sleeves that were too short, his gray hair thin, his face deeply creased, his nose mapped with blue veins. Our paths had crossed before, when a divorce stakeout I was doing at a motel on Sunset got in the way of Haggerty's drug stakeout.

Beside him was a short woman with a Mets cap over a shock of red hair. She wore a *Flames of Desire* jacket, and a headset dangled from her neck, wired to a radio on her belt.

Haggerty said, "Lieutenant, this is Betty Murphy. She's the first assistant director on the movie. I've gotten her statement, but she wants to run something by you."

Murphy stuck her hand out to Charlie and said, "I'm wondering if I can release some of my people, Lieutenant."

"Might be a little bit yet. I'll give you a heads up."

She nodded and looked in my direction. "Hi. I think we've worked together. You're an actor, right?"

"Sometimes."

"Collins? Did you work on *Hell House*? I was a production assistant on it. It got me my Directors Guild card."

"I'm glad it did somebody some good. I don't even remember what I did on it."

"You were one of the bikers. Part of a gang that was roughing up some little hash house out in the boonies."

"That's right," I said. It had been one in a long line of cinematic gems I'd appeared in. I'd worn pounds of leather and choked on exhaust fumes.

"You working on this picture, too?" Haggerty said. "Or are you just here to fuck up the investigation?" He uttered a small laugh that turned into a hoarse cough, and he covered his mouth with a dirty handkerchief.

"Collins has been retained by the movie's insurance company," Charlie said. "And he knew the victim."

As Haggerty said "Huh" and walked off, Betty Murphy said, "It was nice to see you again, Mr. Collins."

"Likewise."

She flashed us a little salute and headed off.

"What does a first assistant director do?" Charlie asked.

"They're like a first sergeant in the Army. Run the day-to-day operation, keep the production on schedule. Somebody has a problem, the first AD is the person to go to."

"They'd have access to the trailers?" Charlie motioned for me to follow him, and we started walking toward Elaine's trailer.

"Absolutely."

"Who else?"

"The first AD's assistants."

"How many of those are there?"

"Depends. If you get a call sheet, it'll tell you how many are on the crew." I pulled out my Chubby's call sheet again and showed him. "On my commercial shoot, Penni Wilson is listed as the AD, and she's only got one assistant. A movie shoot is usually going to have more than one."

"Where would I get a call sheet for this thing?"

"Betty Murphy would have them."

Charlie nodded as we stepped over the yellow tape. "Who else has access?"

"Transportation."

"What's that?"

"Teamsters. They're the guys who open up the trailers in the morning, clean them, stuff like that. Wardrobe people also have access."

"So my goddamn crime scene, if that's what I've got, is a regular Chinese fire drill? People going in and out all morning?"

"Could be."

Charlie shook his head as he opened the door of the trailer. "Well, hell, we might as well join the party. Come on, there's a couple of things in here I want to ask you about."

Chapter Five

Most of the dressing rooms I've had have been of the honeywagon variety, a small, rectangular cubicle with a sink and a commode. Elaine's trailer was out of my league. As I glanced around, I caught a whiff of something and said, "Any of your forensic people smoke cigars, Charlie?"

"I don't think so." He sniffed. "I see what you mean."

I could probably find fifty people on the lot who liked cigars, but Sam Goldberg was the one I'd been with recently. "Was Mr. Goldberg in here this morning?"

"Not to my knowledge. Don't tell me he's also got access to this place?"

"He owns the lot."

"Jesus Christ, we might as well invite the Dodgers and the Lakers while we're at it." He pulled some latex gloves from his pocket and tossed me a pair. "They've been through here and dusted, but you better put these on."

"You're letting a civilian invade your scene?"

"I swear I don't know how you got here." He picked up a framed photograph from a shelf and handed it to me. "Who's that with Weddington?"

I looked at the photo and felt a little catch in my throat. It was a fairly recent shot of Elaine standing next to a tall, dark man with a neatly trimmed beard. Behind them were a house and jacaranda trees.

"His name is Vince Ferraro."

"She involved with him? She remarry?"

"I heard she was living with him, but I don't think she got married again."

"You know where they lived?"

"Nope."

"Who would? The Murphy woman again?"

"If not her, Goldberg's office."

Charlie noted Ferraro's name in his notebook and started walking toward the rear of the trailer. "There's some more back here." He stopped when his phone chirped. "Rivers." He listened, then took the phone away from his ear. "Parker Center. Public Information office. Gimme a minute."

I made a circular motion with my finger, indicating if it was all right to look around.

Elaine had lacked none of the creature comforts afforded a movie star. The furniture was plush and looked comfortable. The kitchen had a CD player, a microwave, some kind of food processor, an espresso machine. I noticed needlepoint and an iPod on the table. I'd never known Elaine to have the patience for needlepoint, but it had been a long time since I'd shared her downtime.

I opened the refrigerator. It contained several bottles of water, seals still intact. A few unopened plastic containers of juice were on another shelf, beside what had been a six-pack of small yogurt cups, of which five cups remained in a plastic yoke. I closed the refrigerator and opened cupboards. Nothing in them except dishes and cans of broth.

The argument could be made that dressing rooms like this are unnecessary except to the vanity of stars. But if you're working on a picture for weeks, as Elaine was used to doing, about the only time you spend at home is to pick up the mail and make sure your key still fits in the front door. And a trailer gets claustrophobic, so the more luxurious the better.

Charlie was still on the phone. He put a hand over it and told me, "They're crawling all over me about a press conference. Take a look at the pictures in the bedroom. See if you can identify anyone. Make sure you don't move anything."

I raised my hand, palm out. "No problem."

I headed for the rear of the trailer. The bathroom was on the right and bore all the evidence of a woman's presence. Makeup brushes and small containers of cosmetics were strewn over the top of the sink cabinet. Rumpled towels hung limply from the shower rod and a couple of items of lingerie lay on the floor. The door of the medicine cabinet was covered with dusting powder. I stuck a finger under the bottom lip and pulled it open. It was empty, not even an aspirin, which told me that forensics had cleaned it out.

I went on to the bedroom. The reality of it finally hit me as I noticed the scent of lilac. For as long as I had known her, Elaine had used a perfume that suggested lilacs. She said it reminded her of the lilac bushes that grew outside her bedroom in Nebraska. When her mother cut huge bouquets for the table, Elaine had had to peek around the flowers to see her father laughing as he passed plates of fried chicken and mashed potatoes. She said the scent of lilacs lingered for days, just as it was lingering now, keeping her presence in the room.

The comforter covering the bed was crinkled where someone had lain. Next to a small indentation on the pillow, the pillowcase fabric was knotted up, as if a clenched fist had held it. On the floor by the bed a square of the carpet had been cut and removed.

A small CD player was on the nightstand. I picked up one of the compact discs that lay near it. She had been listening to Duke Ellington: *Money Jungle*. Charlie Mingus on bass and Max Roach on the drums. I'd sat up with it many times. We had still had a few things in common.

Also on the nightstand were several pictures of Elaine with various people, some of whom I recognized. Most were actors, smiling on movie sets.

I opened drawers of a small bureau and found a few pieces of lingerie and some white athletic socks. A copy of the screenplay of *Flames of Desire* lay on top of the bureau. Its pages were dog-eared and covered with scraps of Post-It notes.

The closet contained two blouses on padded, cloth-covered hangers, jeans, pressed slacks. On a shelf above the hangers, next to a folded sweatshirt and a baseball cap, was a small suitcase that I pulled down and opened. Except for a sweater and a light windbreaker, it seemed to be empty. I ran a hand through one of the zippered sleeves and felt something. When I pulled out a small picture frame and turned it over, I sank onto the edge of the bed, biting my lower lip to fight the tears that flooded my eyes.

It was a picture of Elaine and me on Catalina Island, the Avalon Casino framed behind us. We had been celebrating one of our birthdays, drinking, laughing, and vowing this was the end of birthdays in our lifetimes. In fact, we had had such a good time we had briefly considered becoming Catalinians, at least on a part-time basis. On the island we had seen our first buffalo, part of a herd that had been brought over years ago by Hollywood to add color to *The Vanishing American*, then left behind to become tourist attractions.

What year was that, I wondered. When I turned the picture over and slipped it from its frame a three-by-five card slid out and dropped to the floor. "December 1997" was scrawled on the back of the photo in Elaine's handwriting. I picked up the fallen card. On it were six phone numbers, with a set of initials next to each number. They also seemed to be in Elaine's hand.

I heard Charlie winding up his phone conversation, so I jotted down the initials and numbers in my notebook. I put things back as I'd found them and walked down the hallway.

Charlie closed the phone and shook his head.

I peeled off my latex gloves. "Get everything straightened out?"

"Ah, Christ. You recognize anyone in those pictures back there?"

"A few actors. They looked like they were shots from films she worked on."

He nodded and fumbled in his pocket for a cigarette. "I better go talk to those goddamn reporters."

Chapter Six

Betty Murphy was ending a conversation over her headset. "I can't release her until I get an okay from LAPD. Tell her to chill out. And Leslie, tomorrow morning Dean wants all department heads in the production office at eight. We have to figure out what the hell we're going to do." She signed off and turned to me. "We're in kind of a circus here."

"I was wondering if I could get a copy of today's call sheet."

"Sure." She unfolded the oblong tablet under her arm and handed me a sheet of paper.

"Got time for a couple questions?" I gave her one of my business cards.

"All right."

We headed down the line of trailers, which included hair and makeup and actors' digs. On one door a strip of masking tape said "Marsha," identifying the character rather than the person playing her. A stranger wandering past would be less likely to poke his nose into a trailer with a character's name than a famous actor's. I looked at the call sheet and saw that "Marsha" was Janet Moreland. The name was familiar but I couldn't put a face to it.

We went into a production trailer a couple doors down. It was crowded with desks supporting computers and other office gear. Large manila envelopes hung on a wall, each bearing the name of a different department. Art direction, wardrobe, and the like. Memos and other correspondence protruded from them. Off to my left were more desks and the door leading to another, smaller office. In the center of the trailer sat a sofa, to which Betty gestured.

"You need coffee? Water?"

"I'm good, thanks." I sank down into the sofa. Betty tossed my business card and her tablet on a desk and straddled a wheeled chair. "Shoot."

"Tell me what happened this morning."

"Elaine was doing a scene with Josh Bauer. A love scene. One of her eyelashes kept coming loose. Then she blew a line, and Josh lost it. She lit into both him and director, and then stormed off, so we broke for lunch. We found her in her trailer about an hour later."

"Who found her?"

"Leslie Anderson, my first assistant."

"Anybody else in her trailer?"

"Just Elaine's assistant, Jody Burgess."

"Does she have a key?"

"He. Jody generally watches her trailer when Elaine's not there. He's a marathon needle-pointer."

"Would Jody lock the door if he left?"

"He's supposed to, sure." The phone on her desk rang and she picked it up. She consulted her metal notebook and relayed a name to the caller, then hung up. "Look," she said, "the police aren't telling me anything, but they're acting like this was a crime. That somebody—"

"They don't know. So they're digging. Me, too, but for the insurance guys." I waited until she nodded, then said, "I understand Elaine was suffering from some sort of ear infection?"

"Yeah. She'd been bothered with it for a few days."

"That the only thing bothering her?"

"Well—" Betty paused and toyed with the brim of her Mets cap. "She was having trouble with the guy playing opposite her. This Josh Bauer."

I looked down at the call sheet. "What kind of trouble?"

"She didn't feel he was fully committed. The kid's young, not as disciplined as Elaine was."

"Was she having trouble with anyone else in the company?"

"A lot of people probably considered her difficult."

"Did you agree?"

"Not really. Elaine had quite a career. Been around for a while. She was a pro, and expected people to be the same."

"Had you worked with her before?"

"No, but I had heard stories. Believe me, there were plenty of them." She removed the cap, ran a hand through her hair. "What about you? Lieutenant Rivers said you knew her?"

"I used to be married to her."

"Oh!" Her mouth froze. "That's awful. I'm sorry."

"It had been a while. Had Elaine worked with anyone in the cast before this?"

"I think Janet mentioned something one day about having been on another project with Elaine a few years ago."

"Janet Moreland?"

"Yeah."

"Why do I know that name?"

"She's married to Hal Reese. Heard of him?"

"The City Councilman?"

"You got it."

I had heard of Councilman Reese. He was making a run for mayor, a staunch conservative taking on the liberal left personified by Hollywood. Funny that his wife should be among the enemy. I consulted the call sheet. "According to this, Moreland wasn't called until right after lunch."

"Right. I had to bump her call back an hour since we were running late. Dean wanted to finish with Elaine and Josh before we got to her."

"And she was at home?"

"I don't know. I called her on her cell."

"Is she still on the lot?"

"Yeah, she's the one I was talking about to my assistant. The one who wanted to know if she could leave."

"Do you think I could talk to her?"

"I don't see why not. She and Madeline are in her trailer."

"Madeline?"

"Madeline Schmidt, Janet's coach, or guru, or something." She rolled her eyes.

"A hanger-on?"

"Something like that. Janet studies with her. Come on, I'll walk you over there. Break the ice."

"One more thing. Can you give me Elaine's address?"

She slid open a drawer in a file cabinet, pulled up an envelope and gave me a phone number and address out in Woodland Hills.

"Thanks," I said. "Looks like you've had your hands full."

"It's not exactly been a day at the beach. I'd make a crack about temperamental actors, but considering the company I'd better not."

"Not me," I said. "I've never had that kind of billing. Call me a blue-collar actor, always grateful for the work. Besides, I come from the Spencer Tracy school of acting."

"Which is?"

"He pretty much said just learn your lines and don't bump into the furniture."

She laughed, picked up her tablet and pushed open the door to the trailer. "And he won two Oscars," she said. "There's a lesson there somewhere."

Chapter Seven

We came out of the production trailer and walked back toward the sound stage. I said, "I imagine Haggerty already asked you this, but would you mind telling me where you were up until the time you broke for lunch?"

"On stage, except for a trip to the john."

"What time would that have been?"

She thought for a moment, then consulted her schedule. "It must have been around nine o'clock. Elaine and Josh were called to the set at eight-thirty. They were still lighting the set so I popped out for a couple of minutes."

"Eight-thirty was the first call?"

"Right. There were two setups scheduled before lunch."

"And those were just with Elaine and this Josh Bauer, right?"

"Correct. Only the two of them in both scenes."

We walked up to the door of the trailer that had "Marsha" on it. Betty stood next to the short set of stairs, reached up and knocked. After a moment the door swung open and a woman stuck her face out. She had black hair and tortoise-shell glasses.

"Hi, Madeline," Betty said. "This is Eddie Collins. The insurance company has hired him to investigate Elaine's death. He'd like to ask you and Janet some questions if you don't mind."

"A private detective?"

"Lieutenant Rivers said it was okay."

"The police have already questioned us."

"Yes, ma'am," I said. "I won't take much of your time. I'm just trying to get some basic facts."

She spoke over her shoulder, then pushed the door wide and let us in.

Another woman rose from behind a small table. She was in her late thirties, early forties. She was slender and blond, around five-eight, and seemed to be brimming with confidence.

"I'm Janet Moreland," she said, offering her hand. She wore a black leather jacket, black turtleneck, jeans tucked into expensive looking knee-high leather boots.

I recognized her now from news footage about the mayoral race. I had a vague notion I'd seen her in movies, too, but that was as far as it went.

"Eddie Collins," I said. Her handshake was firm. I doffed my hat and glanced around. The accommodations weren't as spacious as Elaine's but looked comfortable. "I enjoy your work," I said. She had no idea whether I'd ever seen her on the screen. In this town flattery is as cheap as day-old bread.

"Thank you," she said. "This is my associate, Madeline Schmidt." She gestured to the woman who had let us in.

Betty said, "Janet, I think the police are almost done in there."

"I certainly hope so. I've got a sick daughter at home, and a son who suddenly thinks the universe revolves around him."

"I'll let you know the minute I hear anything."

"Thanks, dear. Do you know what tomorrow's call is? Or do we even have a call, considering what's happened?"

"I'm not sure yet. I'm going to have to phone you later."

"You know there's a twelve hour turnaround?"

"Yes, Janet, I am aware of that."

"And I'm still having trouble with that costume for the banquet scene. I've told wardrobe three times it doesn't fit properly."

"I'll talk to them again."

Betty made a beeline out the door, and Janet Moreland focused on me. "I'm curious. Why does the insurance company hire a private investigator?"

"The people that put up the completion bond are worried. Since I sometimes work in the business, they hope I have an insider's eye."

"What do you do? In the business, I mean?"

"I'm an actor."

"Oh, really?" Her eyes lit up in surprise. "And what would we have seen you in?"

"Probably nothing you would remember. Third cop from the left, that sort of thing. Mostly day player stuff."

"So being a detective is just a hobby?"

"Actually, the acting is becoming the hobby. The times between jobs are getting longer as the years go by."

"Yes, I know what you mean." She smiled. Her clothing and the car sitting outside, a newer Mercedes, told me she had no idea what I meant. I was willing to bet a Chubby's Chicken residual she hadn't seen an unemployment claim in years. "Whatever happened to Elaine—I have trouble believing it. How can we help you, Mr. Collins?"

"I understand that you weren't called until this afternoon. Is that correct?"

"Yes."

"Can you verify your whereabouts this morning?"

"Am I a suspect?"

I tried a smile. "If there was a crime, everyone's a suspect. Even the butler."

"And the maid, I suppose." She looked to Madeline and the two of them exchanged smiles. Their confidence bordered on arrogance. "I took the two children to school at 7:30—"

"You have more than two children?"

"Excuse me?"

"You just said your daughter was sick. She went to school anyway?"

Her eyes narrowed slightly at the interruption. "I'm sorry, Mr. Collins. Obviously I misspoke. Stephanie stayed home. I have a housekeeper who looks after her. My neighbor's car is at the mechanic's, so I took her son with me. He and Anthony go to the same school. So, as I was saying, I took the two children to school at 7:30."

"And where did you go then?"

"I dropped into the gym for a short workout, and then I was with Madeline the rest of the morning until coming to the studio."

"Where do you work out?"

"A 24 Hour Fitness in Westwood. On Sepulveda just below Santa Monica."

"And what time were you there?"

"Approximately eight to nine, give or take a few minutes."

"I imagine someone there can verify that?"

"Yes. The staff knows me personally. I've been a member for several years."

"And then you and Madeline met somewhere?"

"Actually Janet came to my place," Madeline chimed in. "We worked on some of the material she was going to be shooting this afternoon."

I turned to Madeline and said, "So you were home all morning?"

"That's correct."

"Betty told me that you're Janet's teacher."

"Yes. She's studied with me for several years. We utilize the principles of Sanford Meisner. Along with The Chubbuck Technique. Are you familiar with those, Mr. Collins?"

"Afraid not," I replied. I'd heard of Meisner, but for all I knew, the Chubbuck Technique could have been the one I used on the Chubby's Chicken commercial. No need to apply to the Spencer Tracy school of acting with these two. I had a hunch there was much discussion of motivation, sense memory, magic circles and all the rest of the mumbo-jumbo associated with what basically comes down to learning one's lines and not bumping into the furniture.

"Well, Mr. Collins," Madeline continued, "I'm always on the lookout for new students."

"I'll consider it. So, Madeline, you're given access to the production?"

"That's written in my contract," Janet said. "Maddie's help is invaluable to me."

I nodded. "And you both came to the studio together?"

"That's correct," Janet said.

"Which is normally the case?"

"I don't drive, Mr. Collins," Madeline said. "So, yes, that is normally the case."

"I see." I turned to Janet. "Betty told me you worked with Elaine prior to this."

"Three or four years ago. Briefly. An unforgettable thing for Paramount, I'm afraid."

"How did the two of you get along?"

"Except for a small disagreement, we enjoyed working with each other."

"What was the disagreement?"

"Oh, something insignificant, really. A scene between us wasn't working. It had more to do with the writing and the directing actually."

"Were you getting along on this picture?"

"Absolutely. Since Betty has been such a font of information, you've probably heard that Elaine had been a little . . . disagreeable, I guess is the best way to put it. She hadn't been feeling well. You've no doubt heard grumbling from others on the set about her."

"Not really. But would the complaints be a reason for someone to kill her?"

"I wouldn't have thought so." She stared at me. "It's hard enough to believe that that's what happened. If you're thinking either one of us could have done it, you're looking in the wrong direction. Since you've been around the business for a while, Mr. Collins, you know that actors have pretty thick skins. Temperamental stars are a dime a dozen. Besides, as I've just told you, Madeline and I have air-tight alibis."

"So it would seem." I smiled at her. "I imagine the butler and the maid would say the same thing."

"*Touché.*"

A sudden knock from outside roused Madeline. As she swung the door open, Betty Murphy leaned inside. "Sorry to barge in, guys. The police have given the okay to release everyone."

"Thank you, Betty."

"Your call is ten a.m. tomorrow."

"And what will we be doing?"

"That hasn't exactly been determined. But we should know by the time you get here."

"I'll be here, Betty." Janet Moreland extended her hand to me. "A pleasure meeting you, Mr. Collins."

"Thanks for your time." I handed her one of my cards. "Feel free to give me a call if you think of anything we haven't covered."

She laid the card on the table. "Of course."

"Nice to meet you, Madeline." I extended my hand to her.

"Likewise. When I get home I'm going to the Internet Movie Data Base and see where those third cops from the left appeared."

I chuckled. "You won't be impressed."

"Maybe some coaching could resuscitate that career, Mr. Collins. The offer still stands." She smiled and shook my hand.

I spotted Charlie Rivers huddled with a crime scene technician at the rear of the forensics van. "Still here?" he said. "I'm going to have to fire my detectives and put you on the payroll."

"I think they're safe, Charlie." I looked at the plastic boxes of evidence and could see pill bottles and toiletries. "Is that all from her trailer?"

"Yeah. It's a mini-pharmacy. Prozac, Valium, estrogen, you name it. The lab guys took practically everything that was in a tube or a bottle. And everything that was open in the refrigerator."

He lifted the lid of an ice chest and I could see Styrofoam containers and clear-plastic take-out boxes with the remnants of salads and other food inside them. In one bag was a companion to the yogurt containers I had seen in the refrigerator. A plastic spoon nestled beside it.

I pointed to another bag. "What's that?"

Charlie picked it up. The bag contained a small brown bottle that was closed by an eye-dropper. Beside the bottle was a box with a pharmacist's label. "Depending on what the tox screens show, this may be a murder weapon. The bottle is supposed to contain medication for an ear infection. We'll see."

"Is it a prescription medication?"

"Filled from a pharmacy in Westwood. Her assistant, this Jody Burgess, picked it up."

I stared at the evidence bag until Charlie noticed and poked me on the shoulder. "What's the matter? You see a ghost?"

"When I was in Goldberg's office, he was putting some kind of medicine on a sore tooth. It looked like the same bottle, Charlie."

"Are you sure?"

"It was this size, brown, with an eye-dropper."

"Interesting. Tell me, did Goldberg and Weddington get along?"

"She worked for him for years. They must have."

"Unless they hated each other for years." He looked at me doubtfully. "You gonna be all right?"

"Yeah."

"My ex and I don't exactly see eye to eye, but she's still my ex. You know?"

"I'll be fine, Charlie," I told him.

Chapter Eight

It was pushing seven p.m. when I stepped off the elevator on the fifth floor of my building. The bottom of the paper bag with the burger and fries was beginning to grow a grease spot that would have been right at home on the hallway carpet. Alex Ford has been my landlord for ten years. Every time a tenant mentions that maybe it's time to put down new carpet, Alex deflects the suggestion by reminding us of the time he worked on this or that picture, that he knew so-and-so or had appeared with ol' what's-her-name. He came out here from New York during the heyday of live television and put his money into real estate. I'm not sure this particular building qualifies as such. But it provides me with both office and living quarters.

A Russian doctor, a men's magazine called *Pecs and Abs*, and the Elite Talent Agency are my closest neighbors.

As I juggled the burger and fries with a bag containing beer, a client of Elite came out of the office. She was all legs and had bumps and curves. She smiled at my struggles to fit my key in the door.

"You need some help, Mr. Collins?" she asked, in a voice that was mostly whispers. She grabbed the bag with the beer, and I found the lock and got the door open. As I retrieved the bag, her long fingers brushed my wrist.

"Thanks. Never enough hands when you need them," I said.

"I know. I run into that with every guy I meet."

She went down the hallway, and I went into the office and dumped the bags on a corner of my assistant Mavis's desk, next to the computer on which she spends most of the day buying and selling collectibles online. Both of us realized early that Collins Investigations wasn't going to occupy her full time.

I popped a beer, tackled the burger and pushed the message button on the blinking phone. Chubby's Chicken said I had an eight o'clock call at the campfire. Not bad. The second message was from Morrie Howard, my agent. He repeated my call-time for the commercial and said he had an audition lined up for me for an industrial film in Modesto, sponsored by the California Prune Growers. "Listen, Boobie, it's a week's work. Double scale. Not bad, huh? Modesto is swingin'."

Everybody was "boobie" to Morrie. I've been with him six years. While he hasn't made me a household name, he accepts the fact that I'm not willing to go out on the hustle for every job that comes along. So I questioned why he thought he could slip this Modesto thing by me. My stomach couldn't handle two consecutive jobs dealing with food, especially one with prunes. I called Morrie back, got his machine, confirmed the eight o'clock call and told him I would pass on the prunes.

I pulled out the note I'd made of phone numbers I'd found hidden in Elaine's trailer. Six sets of initials and six phone numbers without area codes. No telling where they were. There was a time when the only area codes for greater Los Angeles were 213 and 818. Now the city is adding them faster than Liz Taylor went through husbands.

Mavis could play with the numbers online tomorrow. I took a stab at the one next to "AC," putting "213" in front of it. A masculine voice with a thick Hispanic accent mumbled, "*Holla.*"

"Yeah, is Elaine there?"

"Who?"

"Elaine. I'm a friend of hers. She gave me this number."

"Choo got the wrong number. There ain't no fuckin' Elaine here." The phone slammed down.

The next set was "DE." All I got was an answering machine for a post-production house. It said to leave my name and number and they'd catch me on the backside, whatever that was.

I dumped the dinner trash and went into the next room. My old desk had two chairs in front of it with the same worn look of the four-drawer file cabinet that sat in a corner. A closet had been converted into a co-educational restroom. An alcove held a small fridge, microwave, coffee machine and cupboards where Mavis stored her trading paraphernalia. I kept my nose out of the cupboards on her command. She could have a collection of shrunken heads in there for all I knew.

Behind my desk hung a beaded curtain separating the office from my living quarters. The rooms looked as lonely as an Orange County Democrat. I flicked on a floor lamp and saw the Murphy bed still in its supine position, left that way in my haste to get to the shoot that morning.

Lining the walls were shelves bearing too much electronic equipment, CDs and movies on tape and DVD. Some months ago I had come up with the notion of collecting all the Academy Award-winning films. The library now amounted to several hundred titles. I had started watching the winners by year and had gotten to *The Grapes of Wrath* from 1940. Jane Darwell won for supporting actress, and John Ford had gotten his second for direction.

I opened a set of French doors and stepped out onto my miniscule balcony that overlooked a stretch of Hollywood Boulevard. The landing was big enough for a plant or two, but plants always seemed to come to my place and die.

Die. The word stung

I still found it incredible that a life that had been a part of mine for so long had ended.

Down on the boulevard a leather-clad young man was aiming a camera at a tall young woman. Another man held a spotlight on her as she mugged and goofed off for the lens. Anything for the camera, the great window to fame and fortune. The endless baring of the soul to feed an insatiable need for what? Acceptance? Self-esteem? I wondered where she was from. The Midwest, the South? Maybe

Oklahoma, another in a long line of Okies? The fine old character actor John Carradine had played Jim Casy in *The Grapes of Wrath*. When the Joads asked him if he was coming along to California, he said that he'd like to, because "there's somthin' goin' on out there in the west, and I'd like to try and learn what it is." I wondered if this young woman flirting with the camera would learn what it was.

The list of initials and phone numbers was bugging me.

I went back to Mavis's desk. "JH" was next up. I opted for the 310 area code and dialed. On the second ring, a male voice said, "Yeah, honey, I'm on the way."

After a moment, I said, "I didn't know you cared."

There was a pause. "Who is this?"

"I'm calling for Elaine Weddington."

Another pause and the voice said, "How did you get this number?"

"She gave it to me. I'm trying to get hold of her. This is JH, right?"

"I don't know any Elaine!" His voice was panicked. He broke the connection.

I went back to my balcony and enjoyed the thought that somewhere out there in the mist I had opened a door and released a skeleton. It was dancing and rattling in the cool damp of what was sure to be a restless night for JH.

Chapter Nine

It's just possible I may have done some of my best acting that morning around Chubby's campfire. I reached deep into my bag of Stanislavskian tricks, called up some sense memories and pretended the chicken tasted like jello. For the most part it worked. I managed to hold out until it was time for the spit-bag.

My li'l partner, Sidney, on the other hand, sat on his clean rock, grinnin', chewin', and spittin' like he was about to be inducted into the Cowboy Hall of Fame.

Gil Crawford our director was also a wonder of transformation. He acted like he had become a protégé of Frank Capra. Clapping people on the back, laughing, and even yelling "cut" before Chubby's Cajun Deelux sauce began to take on a life of its own. The combination of happy campers made for an uneventful half day, and we were done with the roundup by eleven o'clock.

I'd gotten Mavis started on the phone numbers. At the first bistro I spotted on Sunset, I went in for a beer to wash away the taste of chicken. Mavis answered the office line on the second ring.

"I checked those numbers in a reverse directory," she said. "Except one I didn't have to do. The number next to 'RS' belongs to Vandalia Bond and Casualty."

"You're sure?"

"Sure as I'm sitting here."

Chad Wentworth of Vandalia was going to have to tell me who "RS" was, if anyone there had those initials.

"What about 'JH'?" I asked.

Mavis gave me the address of a law firm in Century City. "AC" and "DE," which I'd called last night, matched up with an Alex Chavez and Deadline Effects. Sooner or later, six numbers would yield six identities. Whether they were connected except on Elaine's list I didn't know.

"Listen, Google Janet Moreland and Hal Reese."

"The guy who's running for mayor?"

"That one. She's an actress."

"Okay." Mavis started to tell me for the second time that morning how sorry she was about my ex. Before she could get going, I said I would check in later and ended the call.

Architecturally speaking, the Los Angeles Basin reminds me of a polygraph test. The interrogation goes along smoothly. Then all of a sudden the person in the hot seat lies through his molars. The needle goes blip. Little horizontal skyscrapers spurt out. The Wells Fargo Tower, blip; Glendale, blip; Mid-Wilshire District and Santa Monica, blip blip. Century City, with its twin towers, sets the machine jumping.

The lobby of the building where "JH" hung his shingle oozed new money and clout. Mavis had told me the suite number was 1850. I stood in front of a huge wooden slab covered in glass, which listed the building's occupants. Next to 1850 was Benson and Hodges, Attorneys-at-Law. Very cute.

Places like this always make me uncomfortable. I was out of my ZIP Code. Not too long ago, I had auditioned for a movie in one of these blips. When I was through, the director and two stoic producers looked at me like I had just interrupted their afternoon. I asked them if it had been a difficult funeral, which didn't lighten their load or get me the part.

Suite number 1850's reception area had the regulation over-stuffed leather and ferns. An attractive, bespectacled woman sat behind a desk, clicking away at a keyboard. I said, "I'd like to see Mr. Hodges."

"Do you have an appointment?"

"No, but I'm expected."

"Whom shall I say is calling?"

"Eddie Collins."

"And to what is this in reference?"

"I was referred by Elaine Weddington."

She pushed a button and relayed the message.

A door was flung open and the anonymous JH suddenly had an identity. He was a small man with pasty soft skin. He wore horn-rimmed glasses. Blond hair on the top of his head had begun to thin.

I flashed him a little wave and smiled. "We spoke last evening?"

"Come in," he barked. It was the voice I had heard on the phone.

I went into his office. Most of it looked out over Santa Monica Bay. The requisite certificates hung on one wall. His desk dwarfed more leather furniture. He slammed the door and marched behind the desk. "Who the hell—?"

"You got a first name?" I said.

"Jeremy Hodges, Attorney-at-Law."

I pulled my license and tossed it on his desk. He picked it up, looked at it, then at me, and handed it back.

"What can I do for you, Mr. Collins?"

"I'm investigating the death of Elaine Weddington."

"With a PI license? You don't have the authority to do that."

I caught the smugness at the corners of his mouth.

"Okay, Counselor. Let's try it this way. I've been retained by Vandalia Bond and Casualty. They've put up the completion bond for the picture Miss Weddington was working on. That enough authority for you?"

"What possible reason would Vandalia Bond and Casualty have for questioning me?"

"Yesterday I found your phone number at the scene. I wondered why."

He looked at me for a long moment. "Do the police know about this?"

"You think for one minute I'm going to tell you that?"

Hodges pushed his glasses up on his nose and sank into his chair. "What do you want to know?" he almost whispered.

"Did you know Elaine Weddington?"

"Yes."

"How?"

"We met socially."

"What do you mean, socially?"

"I'm reluctant to tell you that, Mr. Collins."

I looked at the lawyer, debating whether or not I should reach over the desk and tighten the knot of his overpriced silk tie.

"Look, Hodges, you can answer my questions, or I can call the lead detective on the case and tell him I've got a potential suspect. If he puts you in cuffs, all your high-rise neighbors will stick their heads out of their expensive offices, wondering what the hell happened to Mr. Hodges, that clever guy. And your poor little receptionist out there is going to have to answer them all by her lonesome."

Dots of perspiration started to bead on Jeremy's receding hairline as he weighed his options. He drummed his fingers on his leather desk calendar. "All right, Collins. But I hope you'll keep this confidential."

"Depends on what it is. How did you know Elaine Weddington?"

"Actually, we met at the premiere of one of her pictures."

"How'd you manage that?"

"What do you mean?"

"No offense, but movie stars generally don't just rub elbows with casual fans. Did someone introduce you?"

"As a matter of fact, I had invested some money with the studio."

"Which studio?"

"Americana."

"Sam Goldberg's studio?"

"Yes, that's right. I was introduced to Miss Weddington."

"Did you see her beyond just that one time?"

"Yes, a few times. We had dinner together. Drinks."

"What else?"

"Excuse me?"

"Did you sleep with her?"

"I resent that question, Collins. I won't even dignify it with an answer."

I looked at him for a long moment, wondering if I had caught him in a trap. I leaned over and put my arms on his desk. "The police are going to want to know why your initials and phone number were found at the scene of a death, Counselor. All sorts of fascinating scenarios present themselves. Blackmail being one of them. Had you heard from her recently?"

"Listen, it wasn't a big deal. We went out for dinner and drinks a few times. It was very pleasant. I enjoyed her company. That was it."

"You married, Jeremy?"

"Yes."

"Were you married when this was going on?"

He pursed his lips and after a moment said, "Yes."

"Did Mrs. Hodges know about this?"

"No, she did not," he said. He rose from his desk and leaned across it. "And if you divulge any part of this conversation to anyone, I will not only deny it, I will sue you in a court of law."

"As opposed to someplace else?"

He stared blankly.

I said, "By the way, where were you yesterday between the hours of seven a.m. and two p.m.?'

"In court. Downtown. You can check it."

At Santa Monica and Sepulveda, I caught a call from Mavis, who told me Betty Murphy was looking for me. When I reached her, Murphy said, "I remembered something weird I thought you should know. How about Musso & Frank's at two?"

Chapter Ten

I couldn't imagine Elaine spending time with someone like Hodges. He wasn't her type. And he was married. Had this been going on while we were together? While she was living with Vince Ferraro?

I was also struck with the fact that she had been introduced to Hodges after his investment in Sam's movies. Was it a *quid pro quo*? Back a motion picture and spend time with a movie star?

I was in the neighborhood of the 24 Hour Fitness Club Janet Moreland had mentioned, ahead on the right, a block and a half south of Santa Monica. The walls inside were mirrors, in front of which hunks of all shapes flexed, posed, and strutted. Going full tilt, treadmills and exercise bikes made me tired just watching.

A cute little brunette behind a receptionist's counter with Steffi on her name tag smiled and said, "Hi, are you interested in a membership?"

"Not today, I'm afraid. But I am wondering if you could give me some information."

"Sure thing."

"I think a friend of mine is a member. I was supposed to meet her here yesterday, but I got my wires crossed and was late. Could you tell me if she showed up?"

"What's her name?"

"Janet Moreland."

"Hmmm, I haven't worked here that long so I don't think I know her, but let me ask somebody else." Steffi called over to a finely-chiseled young man sitting behind a desk. "Tony, can you give . . . what was your name again?"

"Eddie."

"Can you give Eddie here some help?"

Tony rose from behind his desk and walked over. His stride oozed testosterone.

"Help you?" His eyes scanned me with a look of disdain. A shapeless blob stood before him, wearing a raincoat and a battered hat. An infidel invading his citadel of pulchritude.

"Do you know a member named of Janet Moreland?"

He thought for a moment and said, "Yeah, I think so. An actress, right?"

"That's the one. As I was telling Steffi, I was supposed to hook up with her here yesterday morning, but I got caught in traffic on the 405. Do you know if she was here?"

"What time?"

"Between eight and nine."

"I couldn't tell you, sir. We had a bit of an emergency in here about that time."

"Oh, really? Someone get hurt?"

"Worse. An elderly gentleman collapsed on one of the treadmills. We had to call an ambulance."

"Oh, no. Was he all right?"

"We don't know. But things were pretty chaotic for a while. She could have been in, but I don't remember."

"I see. Do you have a record of people signing in?"

"We do, but I'm afraid that information is for in-house use only."

"Yes, I suppose." I wasn't going to get anywhere with Tony. "Well, thanks. I hope the gentleman is all right."

"We all do."

"Mind if I take a brochure?"

"Not at all," Steffi said. "I could give you a tour of the facility if you'd like. We have a ninety-day membership special going on right now."

"Maybe some other time, Steffi. Thanks, though."

Chapter Eleven

Musso & Frank's Grill has been on the same spot on Hollywood Boulevard since 1919. It's known for one of the best martinis in town, and my office is near enough that I get to affirm the legend now and then. Under faded wallpaper with sconces illuminating pastoral scenes framed by dark wood, a middle-aged gentleman and a young woman huddled at a table. Otherwise the place was empty except for sentinel-like waiters who stood with napkins over their arms in short red jackets and black bow ties.

I got there a few minutes before Betty Murphy was due. Augie was behind the bar. He went to work on a martini, brought it over. "I was saddened to hear about Miss Weddington, sir," he said softly. His hands were folded respectfully in front of him.

"Thanks, Augie."

"She was a fine lady. I remember with great fondness the laughter the two of you shared with me years ago. Her presence in here shall be truly missed."

Elaine and I had hung out at Musso & Frank's many evenings when we were first married. Augie had been here, just hitting his stride as a mixologist. I knew his regrets were sincere.

"Are you involved in the investigation, sir?"

"I'm looking into it. Had she been in here lately, Augie?"

He thought for a moment. "Two weeks ago, perhaps, for dinner."

"Do you remember who she was with?"

"As a matter of fact, sir, I do. She was accompanied by a gentleman who introduced himself as . . . " He paused and leaned on the bar. "Well, now, that's funny. I seem to have misplaced the name. It sounded Italian, I believe."

"Ferraro? Vince Ferraro?"

He snapped his fingers. "I do believe you're right, Mr. Collins. He seemed to be a very nice chap. It looked like they were thoroughly enjoying each other's company."

"Can you remember anyone else she might have been in here with?"

He took a swipe at the bar with a damp cloth. "I seem to recall a night several months, or maybe even a year ago, when she was in having drinks with a group of gentlemen."

"Did you recognize any of them, Augie?"

He leaned on the bar. "Miss Weddington was making a picture over on the Americana lot, wasn't she?"

"That's correct."

"And the studio head there is a Mr. Goldberg, right?"

"Sam Goldberg, yes."

"He was one of the gentlemen with her. The others I didn't recognize."

My attention drifted to the couple at the table. The age difference between them was considerable. A producer carrying an audition one step further? A "serious" actress establishing a rapport with her director, discussing interior motives and the arc of the character? Over the life of the restaurant, any plot I could think of had played out. Deals made on a handshake. Screenplays getting their first scribbles on gin-soaked napkins.

By three o'clock I decided I'd been stood up. Then Charlie Rivers called me.

"I'm at Americana. You better get over here."

"What's up?"

"Betty Murphy is dead."

Chapter Twelve

A different guard, my chum Jack Simmons, was on duty at the gate. He leaned over to my window with a parking pass in his hand. "You're supposed to drive right over to Stage 7. Keep this with you. It'll get you on every day."

As I reached the *Flames of Desire* production office, I could hear Charlie Rivers before I could see him. I also heard Sam Goldberg. The two were squared off like a pair of portly bookends. Sam's cigar was in danger of poking Charlie's face.

"I'm not telling you how to do your job," Sam roared.

"Well, it sure as hell sounds like it to me," Charlie responded. "I don't want the crime scene contaminated."

"I own the goddamn crime scene!" Sam threw up his arms in frustration and spied me walking up. "Eddie, you talk to him. I'm fed up. 'Contaminate the crime scene.' We're not doing *Doctor Kildare* here, for crissakes." He stomped off a few paces, then turned and walked back to me. "And what the hell are you doing, siccing the cops on me?"

"What are you talking about?"

"I no sooner get in the office this morning than Thelma tells me Rivers here wants to talk to me. Wants to know where the hell my toothache medicine came from. Had I been in Elaine's trailer yesterday morning? On and on. How the hell did he know about me having a toothache if you didn't tell him? I'm being treated like a goddamn suspect."

"Calm down, Sam. They've got to question everybody. You know that."

"I know that? I'll tell you what I know. I know I don't like being treated like a criminal on my own fuckin' lot."

"I smelled cigar smoke in her trailer. The bottle you were using looked like the one they found by Elaine's bed. I thought the lieutenant should know, that's all. No one's accusing you of anything."

"Oh, yeah? Well, it sure as hell doesn't sound like that to me." He shouted at Charlie, "Do me a favor, Lieutenant. Let me know when the hell I can get my goddamn movie back!" With that he was gone.

I asked Charlie, "What did he say about the medicine bottle?"

"Said he picked it up at a Rite Aid near where he lives."

"And was he in Elaine's trailer?"

"Yeah, he told me he came over from his office about nine-thirty to see how she was feeling. He looked in her trailer first, saw that she was on the set, and went back to his office." He shook his head. "Now I just hinted that we might have to shut down the production for a day. He goes ballistic."

"He has no leading lady, no assistant director, and he's still shooting?"

"Guess so. He said two murders would add another two million to the gross."

"Jesus," I muttered. It really wasn't that surprising. This town's embrace of the macabre is legendary. I followed Charlie to the door of the production trailer.

At the stairway, Charlie turned to me. "I don't know if this one fits into your jurisdiction, but you better have a look. Sign in with Jenkins here. And keep your hands in your pockets."

Officer Jenkins handed me a clipboard. I added my name and followed Charlie inside. The body was covered by a sheet. It lay on the same sofa on which I had parked myself yesterday. Several criminologists were still poking around the room. A photographer was taking pictures. The business card I had given Betty Murphy was enclosed in a plastic bag on her desk. A chair had been knocked over and a wastepaper basket next to it was upended. The desk was skewed at an angle. There had been a struggle.

"When did you talk to her?" Charlie said.

"We spoke last evening before I left the lot. Today she said she'd thought of something. I was supposed to meet her at Musso & Frank's."

"What kind of 'something.'?"

"I don't know."

Charlie pointed to a small pillow encased in a plastic bag on the floor. "The killer put a pillow over her face. They wrestled to the sofa. Whoever did it must have been pretty strong. She looks like she was in good shape."

"When was she found?"

"Hour and a half ago."

"Not long after we spoke," I said.

He asked the exact time, which I gave him from the phone. Then he lifted the sheet and showed me a sight that wouldn't go away soon. She was dressed in jeans and a UCLA sweatshirt, which was scrunched up around her neck. Face frozen in terror, mouth agape. Charlie pointed to her hands, which were wrapped in plastic bags. "There's cloth fibers of some kind under her fingernails."

"Who found the body?"

"Another assistant director, Leslie Anderson." He replaced the sheet. "Same one who found the body yesterday."

"Do you have Elaine's tox results?"

"No. But I know we have two homicides."

We stepped out of the trailer and I signed out with Officer Jenkins. Charlie signaled to two of the coroner's people, who carried a gurney inside. A small gathering of onlookers and press had materialized, including brightly dressed extras from the pirate picture. There was a little ruckus as a cop tried to keep a young woman from slipping under the yellow tape.

Charlie lit a cigarette. "Guys with PhDs say the killer is part of the crowd watching a murder scene. Figure they want to see the result of what they've done. Challenging someone to spot them, I guess."

"I'd want to get the hell away from the scene," I said.

"I'm with you."

He chuckled. "You hungry?"

"No, but I could use a drink."

Chapter Thirteen

A place called Sally's was Charlie Rivers's choice. He got there twenty minutes after me, pulling off a wet slicker as he came down the alley between a counter and a line of booths. A door at the rear led to a bar, out of which leaked jukebox noise. I was halfway back along the booths. Charlie sat down.

The waitress named Nancy sauntered over and set a glass of water in front of him. "Something to drink?"

Charlie ordered a light beer and I got a refill on my bourbon.

As she left, Charlie opened his menu. "Tell me again what Murphy said on the phone."

"Next to nothing. That she'd remembered something."

"Could someone have been there when you called?"

"It's possible."

He pulled out his notebook and made some notes for himself. "Who usually has access to that trailer?"

"The director, unless he's got his own office. Murphy's assistant directors. Secretaries and other production people. Gofers, messengers, people like that."

"So anyone could have been there."

"Or come in after we talked. Do you have the call sheet for today?"

He pulled the sheet from a pocket. "Looks like twenty extras called for six o'clock. The Moreland woman and Josh Bauer at ten."

Raising my glass, I remembered something Betty Murphy had said last night. I told Charlie, "Murphy said she wanted all the department heads for an eight o'clock meeting to figure out what they were going to do. Is there a specific scene or scenes slated?"

He looked at the call sheet and said, "TBA. What about those extras? Would they have cause to be in Murphy's office?"

"I doubt it," I replied. "An AD wrangles them. They're usually sequestered in a holding area. In a tent or a corner of another sound stage."

He made notes and drank beer.

"Do you think Goldberg would have a motive for killing Weddington?" he said.

"I can't think of one," I said. "Elaine's pictures made money for him. Unless there was something in their past."

"Like what?"

"I have no idea. What about Jody Burgess?"

"His prints are all over the place."

"Including the medicine bottle?"

"The bottle was wiped clean." Charlie looked across the table at me. "Seems your ex wasn't well-liked around the set. That surprise you?"

"Somewhat. She had some Italian in her, and she had a temper, but there was no malice."

"You two didn't have kids, did you?"

I shook my head. "Didn't seem the wise thing to do with two careers trying to take off."

"None of my business, but why did you split?"

"I don't think actors are easy people to live with, Charlie. Two of them is even worse."

"Competition, huh?"

"That, and jealousy. Elaine's career started taking off. Mine sat in idle. I didn't handle it well."

Charlie nodded as if he'd heard it all before.

Chapter Fourteen

It was a fine looking leg, very shapely, encased in a fish-net stocking. A high heel covered the foot. A lampshade with a fringe around it sat on top of the leg. I gazed at the lamp in wonder. It had been waiting for me in the office, along with a note from Mavis explaining it had been just too good a bargain on eBay to ignore. I couldn't disagree with her. It was a replica of the one Darren McGavin ordered from a mail-order catalog in the classic holiday film *A Christmas Story*.

I had been up for a couple of hours, unable to sleep. Visions of Betty Murphy danced in front of me. I sipped on a cup of coffee and waited for Chad Wentworth of Vandalia Bond and Casualty to pick up the phone. Mavis had left a message that he'd been trying to reach me.

No answer from Wentworth.

I went back to the material Mavis had compiled on Janet Moreland. Moreland had put together a pretty good career. She'd gotten a Golden Globe nomination a few years back. News clips about her husband Hal Reese described him as very right-wing politically. Anti-abortion. Pro-guns. Strong national defense. Positions that seemed incongruous in Hollywood. I wondered if Janet Moreland managed to balance Reese and her profession.

I'd drunk my third coffee by the time I reached Chad Wentworth. He wanted me to come over and sign paperwork. I wanted him to tell me who "RS" was. I didn't mention that when we made a date for four o'clock.

I heard Mavis arrive and called, "Good morning." She came in, plugged in the leg lamp, switched it on, and raised an eyebrow at the result. "What do you think? Too gauche?"

"Absolutely not."

This morning she was wearing soft yellows, bringing more color into the room than one man deserved. I decided her husband, Fritz, was a lucky guy.

She'd brought in an *L.A. Times*, which she tossed on my desk. The murder of Betty Murphy had gotten some play. "Are you sure it's healthy hanging around that studio?" Mavis said.

"No, I'm not sure. Sit down, I want your take on something."

She sat.

"I had a talk with Jeremy Hodges. I didn't like something that was between the lines." As closely as I could remember, I repeated Hodges's description of investing in Sam Goldberg's movies and getting introduced to Elaine.

"Is that unusual—for an investor to meet the talent?"

"Not really. But it went further than a meeting. There were dinners—at least—and why would she have Hodges's phone number squirreled away in code behind a photograph? Along with five other numbers? You see where I'm going?"

"Yes, I do, Eddie, but I can't see her making herself . . . available in the way you're implying."

"Why not?"

She shrugged. "It doesn't fit what you've told me about her. In the first place, why would she do it?"

"Maybe somebody had something on her."

"Who? And what?"

"That's where I draw a blank."

"It could be she had something on Hodges," Mavis said.

I hadn't looked at it that way.

"Could Hodges have killed her?" Mavis pressed. "You said the guy was fooling around on his wife. Maybe he thought Elaine was going to blackmail him?"

"Hodges said he hadn't had anything to do with Elaine for several years. And he gave me an alibi that can be checked. Besides, the killer pretty much has to be somebody working on the movie."

"Hodges knows Sam. He could also know somebody else involved with the studio. Somebody on the inside. On the lot."

I thought. "It's worth pursuing. Also, I've got to find out what the other names on the list have to say. Beginning with 'RS' of Vandalia Bond and Casualty."

Mavis went into her office and turned on her computer and said, "Where are you going to be today?"

"At Americana. I'm going to talk to Leslie Anderson."

"Who's he?"

"She. The assistant director who discovered the bodies."

Chapter Fifteen

The red light above the door to Stage 7 had been revolving for almost two minutes. It seemed longer. If I opened the door and went inside, I was likely to draw the wrath of some production assistant. The red light indicates the camera is rolling and the magic is being made. Given the fact that this picture no longer had a leading lady, magic seemed to be the operative word.

A young man wearing pants that ended at his knees and combat boots on his feet peddled up on a bicycle. He took a huge manila envelope out of the bike's basket and joined me under the light.

He looked at my hat and said, "Nice lid."

I looked at his feet and replied, "Nice boots."

I thought for a moment we were going to bond, but that was the extent of it. He now looked at me like I was responsible for his life coming to a standstill. I studied his footwear and marveled at the fact that I had been in the forefront of fashion when I was in the Army.

The light finally stopped. He grabbed the handle of the door and jerked it open. I followed him inside, wondering how soon it was going to be before he became a casting director and I would be auditioning for him.

Activity in the sound stage was centered on a set in the far corner. I headed in that direction, stepping over electrical cables. A lot of people stand around on movie sets. The most popular place is the craft services tables. Munchies abound, running the gamut from squeaky-healthy to double by-pass. Double by-pass was getting the attention. I snatched a donut. No one tried to wrestle it away from me.

I spotted the headphones of an assistant director and was closing in on him when I heard, "All right, lock it up!" A loud bell sounded. Conversations ceased. Activity stopped. All attention was focused on the scene being shot.

Dean Snider, the director, was hunched over in his chair, peering intently at the video monitor in front of him. He was small, furtive-looking, bearded, with glasses. He turned to his right and asked something of a mousy woman with a huge notebook cradled in one arm.

She would be the script supervisor. The notebook contained every page of the screenplay, along with a detailed, by-the-numbers account of every shot. If you've ever watched a western movie and noticed that the clock over the marshal's head covers the span of an hour when the hero is only loading his six-shooter, you've spotted poor continuity and the lack of a good script supervisor.

Extras peppered the interior of a restaurant set. Seated at a table was Josh Bauer. Seated across from him was Janet Moreland. She looked as focused and serious as she had when I interviewed her.

Snider got his answer from his script supervisor. He nodded to his assistant director. Everyone settled. The actor's magical moment came. The lens is your audience and immortality is yours for the taking. The scene played out with no apparent mishaps. Finally the director called "cut" and the two players relaxed.

Like flies to carrion, wardrobe, makeup and hair stylists descended on Bauer, pulling, patting and brushing. Janet Moreland sipped a bottle of water while she was being coddled. She stood next to her guru, Madeline Schmidt, who sat in a canvas chair wearing jeans, a bulky sweater, and a *Flames of Desire* baseball cap. Janet listened intently as Madeline spoke.

I walked up to the fellow with the headphones and identified myself. He told me that Leslie Anderson had been given a couple of days off. He scribbled down her phone number and address.

"What about Jody Burgess?"

"Helping out in wardrobe. There's a costume truck outside." He pointed toward another door.

I was almost there when I heard a shout, "Back to number one, people. We'll go again." Number one meant the beginning of the scene.

Preparation for a movie take is a curious litany of commands. It makes an actor almost feel like he's in the nose cone of a rocket, scared out of his head, about to be launched into the depths of the cosmos. He hears:

"Lock it up!"

(All right, all right, concentrate!)

The bell sounds. The exterior red light begins its revolutions.

(What the hell's the line?)

"Roll sound!"

(Dammit, I should have taken a piss.)

"Speed!"

(What's that extra doing there? Is he going to move?)

"Roll camera!"

(Man, I need some water.)

"Camera rolling!"

(Don't look at her tits. Don't look at her tits!)

"Action!"

And you're out of the chute and into the void, flailing around, taking another stab at fame and fortune, trying not to make a fool of yourself and ruin the take, wondering in the back of your mind why the hell you decided to do this in the first place.

Believe me, I have been there many times.

As I ducked outside, the thought occurred to me that interviewing a murder suspect was perhaps the easier of the two jobs.

Chapter Sixteen

The wardrobe truck was parked next to the sound stage adjoining Stage 7. A corrugated metal ramp protruded from the rear and a stair unit stood below a smaller door toward the front.

I went in the front door. Both sides of the interior held racks of clothing of all kinds. Shoes were lined up on the floor under the racks. Shelves above were strewn with different variations of hats and caps.

Jody Burgess was sprawled in a chair at the front, knees poking from frayed jeans, his black hair slicked back. He wore a sleeveless T-shirt that exposed a tattoo of some Oriental character on his left arm. He put down his needlepoint and stood up.

"What scene you in?" He picked up a clipboard and looked at a roster. "What's the name?"

"Eddie Collins, and I'm not an extra." I took my license out of my pocket and showed it to him. "I'm looking into the Weddington murder."

"Aw, shit, man, I told the cops everything I know."

"I'm sorry I missed it." I straddled a chair, dug out a notebook. "Tell you what. You stitch, I'll ask, you respond, and we'll get through this. Okay?"

It wasn't okay. He sat down but didn't pick up his needlepoint.

"What did you do for Miss Weddington?" I asked.

He scowled. "Everything. I drove her, watched her trailer, ran dialogue with her. Real high-tech, shit work."

"What time did you pick her up on the day of the murder?"

"What does that matter?"

"Humor me. When did you pick her up?"

Sighing, Jody reached for a bottle of flavored water beside his chair. He said, "Six-thirty."

"And came straight here?"

"Yeah."

"And then I understand you picked up a prescription for her?"

"Yeah. After Elaine went to the set, I left to get the prescription."

"Where was the pharmacy?"

"In Westwood. In a strip mall near Wilshire and Beverly Glen."

"The pharmacy allowed someone else to pick up her medication?"

"She worked it out with them. Take a look in her medicine cabinet. She was always sending me over there to get things for her."

"What time did you leave for the pharmacy?"

"Around eight. I came back about eight-thirty, put the drops in the trailer, and then went to craft services to get something to eat. Check with Julie. She'll tell you."

"Where did you put the drops exactly?"

"On her nightstand."

"Were they in a bag?"

"I took them out of the bag and the box they were in and put the bottle on the nightstand."

"What did you do with the bag and the box?"

"I threw them away, for crissakes."

"When you went to craft services, was Miss Weddington's trailer left open?"

"No, I locked it, but that don't mean a damn thing."

"Why's that?"

"Anybody can get through those locks. I've accidentally locked the keys inside and broken in with a hairpin."

"How long were you at craft services?"

"I got back to Elaine's trailer around nine-forty-five."

"And the door was still locked?"

He nodded, took out a pack of cigarettes.

I said, "Do you smoke cigars, Jody?"

"Hell no. I'm even trying to quit these things."

"When you got back from craft services, did you smell cigar smoke in Elaine's trailer?"

He thought for a moment. "Not that I remember. Elaine was dead-set against anyone smoking. She rode my ass pretty hard about it. I had to go outside to light up."

I made a few notes and looked at him for a minute. Even though he was having a bad attitude day, he knew he was in a vulnerable position.

"So between the pharmacist and Elaine using the drops, you're the only one who touched them. Is that right? Did people have a habit of going into the star's trailer?"

He shook his head.

"What happened when Elaine came back to the trailer? About one o'clock, wasn't it?"

"Yeah, something like that. She was pissed, real pissed. She grabbed a container of yogurt out of the refrigerator, ate it right there while she went off on the whole damn picture."

"Who, or what, in particular?"

"Well, she said Josh Bauer was a bad fucking actor. She'd said that before, so that didn't surprise me. But this time she had it in for the director. She said something about everybody ganging up on her."

"She mention any names?"

"Everybody. Janet Moreland, Bauer, the crew. She even had a few choice words for Sam Goldberg."

"Did she mention anybody by the name of Jeremy Hodges?"

Jody thought for a moment. "Not that I remember."

"What did she do when she finished the yogurt?"

"She told me she was going to lie down and put some of those drops in her ear. Said not to wake her. To let the bastards come and get her. Her words, not mine."

"Then?"

"She went into the bedroom and closed the door."

"Did you hear anything later? A scream, a moan, anything?"

"No," he said, looking at the cigarette pack in his hand. "Elaine didn't like my tastes in music, so I always put my headphones on when she was in the trailer."

"So, you're supposed to be her bodyguard, she's back in her bedroom dying, and you're sitting there listening to music?"

After a long moment of staring at me defiantly he said, "Elaine didn't mind me having the headphones on. Besides, how was I supposed to know someone had switched bottles?"

"Why do you say someone switched bottles?"

He looked surprised. "Well, that's pretty obvious, isn't it? The bottle I put down on her nightstand came right from the pharmacy. All the cops crawling around here seem to think there was some kind of poison in the bottle when she used the drops. So it looks like somebody switched the bottle."

I shut my notebook, stood up. "Why couldn't someone have poured out the medicine and substituted the poison?"

He shrugged. "I guess that's possible."

"You could have done that. Is that what you did, Jody?"

He stared at me for a long moment, pursing his lips. "I know I'm probably a suspect in this damn thing. But I had no reason to kill her. She wasn't the easiest person to work for at times, but she was okay, you know? And I was grateful to her. She gave me a break or two along the way."

"What kind of break?"

"She saw to it I was cast in a couple of her pictures. Nothing big, a line or two, but she didn't have to do it. She even tried to get me in on this piece of shit. The part Josh is playing. But the director didn't think I could handle it."

"Could you?"

"Fuck yes! Josh Bauer don't show me nothing."

I asked, "Did you know Betty Murphy?"

"Sure."

"Where were you yesterday when—?"

"When she was murdered? Man, I told the cops all this too. They sent me to Western Costume with the designer. His name is Chris Paxton. We were gone from ten in the morning until about two in the afternoon. You can ask him."

I jotted down the name, handed him one of my cards. "Give me a call if you remember anything else."

Chapter Seventeen

I walked down the ramp of the truck and back into Stage 7. Another scene was being set up and people were milling around. A young woman stood in a little pantry behind the craft services tables. She was chopping up tidbits of healthy snacks. I tapped on the door and said, "Excuse me. Are you Julie?"

"Yes."

I showed her my identification. "My name's Eddie Collins. Wonder if I could ask you a couple of questions?"

She ripped a paper towel from a roll and walked to the entrance of the pantry. "What about?"

"You know Jody Burgess?"

"Yeah."

"He says that on the morning Elaine Weddington died, he came by craft services about eight-thirty. Do you remember seeing him?"

She paused, looked off to the right, eyes scrunched. "That sounds right. He wanted to know if I had any more oatmeal. There wasn't any on the tables."

"You're sure?"

"Yes, I'm sure."

"Okay, thanks."

Outside it looked like more rain. I stopped at Elaine's trailer, stepped over the yellow tape. Nobody seemed to be watching me. I tried the door to the trailer. It was locked. I pulled a fingernail clipper from my pocket, fiddled for a few seconds and the door opened. I pulled the door shut. Jody Burgess had told the truth about that, at least.

As I headed for my car, Josh Bauer came out of the makeup trailer and entered his own. I followed and knocked on the door, introduced myself and said, "Mind if I ask you a few questions? I'm looking into the murder of Elaine Weddington."

"You another cop?"

"Private. I'm on retainer for the insurance company. Mind if I come in?"

"Oh, yeah, sorry." He stepped back and I climbed into the trailer. He had made himself at home—no day player here. A boom box pumped out something sounding of tribal drums. Photographs and CDs filled shelves. A stationary bike took up much of the room. Knowing Sam Goldberg, Bauer had brought the bike from home. Sam wasn't into expensive perks.

Bauer looked like he spent time on the machine. He stood about five-foot eight, well proportioned, dressed in tan Dockers and a red shirt. Tissue protruded from the collar of the shirt to protect it from the fresh makeup.

He silenced the stereo and sat at a table.

"Can I get you something to drink?"

"Thanks. I'm fine." I took out the call-sheet from Elaine's final day. "This says you had a scene with Weddington the morning of the murder. Is that right?"

"Yes. A love scene."

"How did it go?"

"Not well." He described how Elaine's eyelash had come loose and he had broken up and ruined the shot.

"Did she take it out on you?"

"Oh, yeah, big time. She accused me of being a terrible actor. A lousy kisser. She even made some unflattering comments about my . . . privates." Bauer shrugged and chuckled. "I've never had any complaints before, so it wasn't a big deal, really. I know it probably wasn't very professional on my part, but those things happen, you know."

"Had she blown up at you before?"

"Not to that extreme, but there was usually something that set her off in almost every scene we did."

"Had you worked with her before?"

"No, and I was really psyched about getting the job. Good for the resume and the reel, you know? She sure as hell put a damper on that."

"Any idea who might have killed her?"

"I don't suppose it's a secret that she pissed off some people. I'd have a hard time believing anyone would murder her, though."

"What about Betty Murphy?"

"God . . . even less likely. She was a sweet kid."

We went over his time after the crew broke for lunch.

"I wasn't hungry," he said. "I walked around for a while, then came back into the stage and studied lines for another scene that was up that afternoon."

"Anybody see you?"

"Guys on the crew, I guess. I wasn't paying much attention."

"When you took your walk, did you see anything suspicious outside Weddington's trailer?"

"Not that I recall."

"Tell me about Janet Moreland. You have scenes together?"

"Quite a few. She plays my wife in this thing. I'm cheating on her with Elaine."

"How did she seem to get along with Elaine?"

"Not too well, it looked like."

"How so?"

"Professional jealousy, I suppose. On a couple of occasions Janet told me she thought Elaine was doing a lousy job. That *she* should have had the role."

"You agree with her?"

"I knew better than to get into it. Two aggressive women on a movie set in this town?" He laughed.

"What about Moreland's coach, Madeline Schmidt? Do you know her?"

"A little. She keeps after me, telling me I should study with her. I don't know if she's coming on to me or what."

There was a knock on the door, and a young man stuck his head in. "Hey, Josh, you've been in hair and makeup, right?"

"All done. They ready for me?"

"In about fifteen. I'll give you a heads up." The kid backed out.

I stood, collected my hat. "How's the career going? The business treating you all right?"

"Ups and downs. You know. Like everybody else. I had a pilot last spring that I thought would go, but it didn't."

I knew the story all too well. Years ago it could have been me.

I checked in with Mavis, who said that Jeremy Hodges had called. He wanted a meeting.

I got him at his office.

"Do you know where Cheviot Hills Park is?" he asked.

"I do."

"I'm going to lunch in a bit. Why don't I meet you by the Recreation Center, right off Motor?"

Chapter Eighteen

Hodges was sitting at a picnic table under a huge tree. He stabbed at lettuce in a plastic container. A small juice box sat next to it. I straddled a bench and sat down.

He sipped juice through a straw. "I didn't realize you had been married to Miss Weddington," he said. "I'm sorry for your loss, Mr. Collins."

"What did you want to talk to me about?"

"After Elaine . . . ah . . . and I first met, she called me on another occasion wanting legal advice. She was entertaining the thought of bringing suit against somebody. An employer of hers. Sam Goldberg."

"Why did she want to do that?"

He sipped more juice. "I'm not really sure why. She alluded to a contract issue, but basically she just wanted to know what my fee would be. She said she would get back to me on whether she wanted to proceed. I never heard from her again."

"Did you make any attempt to reach her?"

"No. I presumed she had changed her mind."

"When was this?"

"Three weeks ago."

I looked at him. "Why are you telling me this, Hodges?"

"I just thought this information would be something you might need in your investigation."

"And it goes to motive as far as Goldberg is concerned?"

He shrugged. "I'm not an investigator, Mr. Collins."

"Do you know Goldberg personally?"

"I met him a time or two. Cocktail parties. One or two movie premieres. Enough to get bitten by the bug and invest in his films." He rose from the picnic table. "But we aren't close. Well, I must get back. I wish you well in your investigation, Mr. Collins."

Chapter Nineteen

Leslie Anderson lived in Burbank. On the phone she hadn't sounded eager for visitors. I opened the gate of one of those quaint, California courtyards with the little bungalows facing a common strip of lush grass dotted with rose bushes. It was straight out of John Schlesinger's screen version of Nathaniel West's *The Day of the Locust*, arguably the best film ever made about Hollywood. At the top, as William Atherton is looking to rent a cottage in one of these courtyards, he sees Karen Black painting her toenails, pieces of cotton protruding from between her toes like some underdeveloped bunny fuzz.

I didn't see Karen Black. What greeted me was a Shar-pei, one of those wrinkled Chinese dogs, that was relieving himself on the grass. He growled at the interruption. At the other end of the leash, wearing blue Spandex, was a woman as bloated as the Michelin Man.

"Can I help you?" She stumbled as the dog jerked her closer to me.

"I'm looking for Leslie Anderson."

"Last bungalow on your right. And stay off the grass."

Leslie Anderson was tall, maybe five nine or ten. She had long, honey-blond hair pulled behind her ears and held in place with two white barrettes. The strain of the last few days showed in her eyes. "Come in," she said.

She offered me coffee, which I declined, and then went to get herself a cup. I lowered myself onto a sofa full of large, billowy pillows. This was one of the most feminine environments I had seen in a while. Lace curtains covered the windows. Plants hung from hooks in the ceiling. Ornate area rugs covered the floors. Doilies were draped over the arms of the sofa and two overstuffed chairs.

Sprawled across most of a small round table under a window was a large gray cat. It looked up at me, yawned, and replaced its head on its paws. So much for the new guy.

"What's your cat's name?"

"Bugsy," came the reply from the kitchen. "I was a PA on the movie. Warren Beatty lives."

She came back, set her mug on the coffee table, and dropped into one of the big chairs. Bugsy came over and I scratched him on his rump and his tail went up like a starlet's hopes at an audition.

"Thanks for agreeing to talk to me. You've had a rough few days, haven't you?"

"Unbelievable."

"I know the police have been through all this with you, but maybe I might hear something different. Get another take on things."

Bugsy settled into her lap and flicked his tail. She sipped coffee. "Shoot."

"On the day Elaine Weddington was murdered, did anything out of the ordinary happen on the set? Anybody she was particularly upset with?"

"Well, Josh, of course. And the director. And a stagehand who gave her the eye. She hadn't been feeling well for a few days, and I suppose it was making her cranky."

"When you got back from lunch, Betty told you to bring Elaine to the set because they were ready for her. Is that right?"

"Yes."

"Was that what you normally did?"

"Sometimes a PA would do it, but most of the time Betty asked me. She told me that on the pictures she worked . . ." Leslie paused, her lips quivering. She fought back tears and finally yanked a couple of tissues from a box on the table. "Sorry. Betty liked for the stars to be summoned by one of the assistant directors, rather than a production assistant."

"So you're on your way to bringing Elaine to the set. Did you see anyone outside her trailer?"

"No, not then, but I did a few minutes earlier."

"Earlier?"

"When I was coming back from lunch, I saw Janet Moreland and Madeline Schmidt unloading Janet's car."

"What were they unloading?"

"It looked like groceries. At least I saw a bag from Whole Foods. Janet usually brings her own snacks and things like that."

"What time would that have been?"

She thought for a moment and said, "Probably around twelve-thirty, somewhere in there."

"But she wasn't called until two o'clock that day, right?"

"Yes. She said she and Madeline had been running some errands and that they were early. I told her we were a little behind schedule because the production meeting ran long. She said that was fine. She'd be in her trailer."

"Did Janet Moreland and Elaine ever clash over anything?"

"Not to my knowledge. Janet is playing the 'other woman,' so she didn't have much to do with Elaine."

"So you saw Janet and Madeline, and then you went into the stage?"

"First I knocked on Josh Bauer's trailer. I didn't get any answer. I stuck my head inside, but he wasn't there, so I went into the stage. He was already on the set. A little while later, Betty told me that they were ready for Elaine, so I . . ." She stopped and put the coffee mug on the table. "Wait a minute. I just thought of something. After Betty told me to get Elaine, I started to walk off. Then I turned back and told her that Janet was here. That she had just driven up. Betty got a confused look on her face."

"Did she say anything?"

"She said something like, 'Oh, I thought she was here earlier.'"

"What did she mean by 'earlier'?"

"I don't know."

"Was she talking about Janet?"

"She must have been. I mean, Betty ran a tight ship. She always knew what actors were called when. If she had seen Janet before two o'clock, she would have noticed."

"Had you seen Janet earlier?"

"No."

"What about Madeline?"

"No."

Leslie leaned forward and picked up her coffee mug. Annoyed, Bugsy relocated to a large book on the coffee table.

"Leslie, can you think of a reason Janet might have come in early?"

"Not really. She didn't have fittings with wardrobe or anything. She might have wanted to work on lines someplace quiet."

I nodded. She might have indeed. Or wanted to get away from the political campaign at home. It was a stretch to think it had anything to do with Betty Murphy's wanting to meet me at Musso & Frank's.

Chapter Twenty

Chad Wentworth was a Harvard MBA who fit right in at Vandalia Bond and Casualty. He was in his fifties, clean-cut, tanned and very serious.

He looked at me over his tortoise-shelled glasses. "It's my understanding that *Flames of Desire* is still shooting?"

"This morning it was."

"Which is to our advantage, of course. But without a leading lady?" He gave the documents in front of him one final flip-through and slid them across the desk to me. "Sign where I've indicated."

I scanned the contract and began scribbling my name wherever I saw the "x." I said, "Did you ever see that old picture *Elephant Walk*? Starring Elizabeth Taylor?"

"I don't believe so."

"The actress they started shooting with was Vivien Leigh."

He smiled. "Scarlett O'Hara in *Gone With the Wind*."

"Right. But Leigh was having emotional problems during *Elephant Walk* and they replaced her. But if you look close, you can see her in some long shots."

"Interesting. Will Americana try that with *Desire*?"

"Maybe, unless you decide to shut them down. Two murders generate publicity. Sam Goldberg knows the value of that."

"Betty Murphy's death shouldn't impede the production?" Wentworth asked.

"I wouldn't think so."

He folded my copy of the contract and stuck it in an envelope. "What were the circumstances when you worked with us previously?"

"Somebody was stealing handguns from a set a few years ago. They were insured for a pretty penny. We caught some screwed-up kid."

"I see. Then you're familiar with the ropes? Expense accounts? Liabilities?"

"Pretty much, I think."

"Any questions you need answered?"

"I don't think so." I stuffed the envelope into a pocket. "There is one thing, though."

"What's that?"

"This morning I was trying to remember the name of the guy I worked with before. The old contract only had his initials on it. 'RS.' Do those ring a bell with you?"

"I'm afraid not. I've only been with the firm for six months."

"Is there any way to find out his name? He was a helluva of a nice guy. Do you think he's still here?"

Wentworth slipped my contract into a manila folder. He stood and walked to a file cabinet against the wall. "I'm afraid you're going to have to ask Marge, my secretary. She's been here longer than I have." He dropped the contract in the file and slid the drawer shut. "I'll point her out to you."

We walked to the door of his office and he indicated a desk behind which sat a petite young woman. Wentworth and I shook hands and he stepped back into his office.

Marge wore her raven hair in a very becoming short cut. Long sparkling earrings hung from each ear. A deep blue blouse was cinched with a black belt. If Mavis ever threw in the towel, I knew who I wanted to replace her. She looked up from her typing.

"Mr. Wentworth said maybe you could get some information for me."

"I'll sure try. Are you working for us?"

"I've been retained on the Elaine Weddington case."

"Oh, that's a terrible thing."

"Yes. I worked on another case for Vandalia some years ago. I can't remember the name of the person who brought me in, but the initials on the contract were 'RS.' Does that ring a bell with you?"

She furrowed her brow. "I don't think so. Let me get out of this screen." She tapped keys, scrolled down a list of names. "We've got a Rita Salerni and a Rachel Sandler. That's it."

"Nope. We only met one time. I'm sure he was a guy."

"Let me try something else." She tapped some more keys. "Here's a list going back further. There's a Rodney Sullivan, no longer with us."

"That might be him. Do you have an address or phone number?"

She jotted the information on a piece of paper and handed it to me. "Come to think of it, I do remember him. Everybody called him 'Red'—for the hair. He was awfully nice."

Chapter Twenty-One

I stood beside the car at an Arco station, letting the pump run and listening to Charlie Rivers's phone ring. The rain had arrived, and it had an affinity for the back of my neck. I left a message for Charlie to call me at home.

Being a Midwesterner, I like rain. It washes a town down, even Los Angeles.

I needed to talk to Janet Moreland again.

I'd been an actor long enough to wonder about a morning arrival for a two o'clock call. In the theatre, actors will report early. They'll walk the stage, go over lines, and soak up the ambience of the arena in front of them. There isn't much ambience in a motor home.

As soon as I told myself that, I thought of a dozen counter arguments. Moreland might have had a spat with hubby. She might have wanted more study time with coach Madeline. She might have had appointments closer to the studio than to home. Lots of might haves.

But Betty Murphy had wanted to tell me something. It was up to me to figure out what—unless I was misreading that altogether. Maybe she had just wanted to tell me she'd fallen for my baby blue eyes.

It had to happen sometime.

I fumbled for the lock at Collins Investigations when a door down the hallway opened and out stepped Lenny Daye, the editor of *Pecs and Abs*.

"Hey, Eddie," he called, ambling toward me.

"How you doing," I asked, probably squinting. Lenny's wardrobe is as bright as Christmas wrapping paper. His shirt tonight was the inspiration for Steven Spielberg's *The Color Purple*. His shoes were red and almost as high as *cothurni*, those platform shoes Greek and Roman actors wore in the classic tragedies to make them look taller and more heroic. Lenny didn't look heroic. He looked precarious. His jacket was right out of Brando's *The Wild One*. It squeaked as he moved.

"Have you seen Alex lately?" he asked.

"I saw him the other day with the rent checks. What's the matter?"

"I am getting so sick of the smell every time I walk off the elevator, I could puke."

"Somebody's garbage?"

"No, the damn carpet." He stamped on the floor and almost lost his balance. "You think we could twist his arm or some other appendage and get him to get rid of this crap?"

"We can try. Get hold of him and I'll be your backup."

"You got it, honey." He walked to the elevator, every step an adventure.

Since the Russian doctor's greetings consisted of grunts, I welcomed Lenny's banter and the sense of community with at least one of my neighbors.

The answering machine on Mavis's desk was blinking. Her usual note lay next to it. I sat down and punched a button and Charlie's rasp said, "Eddie, Lieutenant Rivers. I did talk to Janet Moreland. She didn't say anything about being on the lot earlier than two o'clock. What's going on? Call and fill me in."

I moved to my desk and dialed the number for Rodney Sullivan. After three rings, a woman answered.

"Rodney Sullivan, please."

"Who?"

"Rodney Sullivan?"

"Nobody by that name here."

"On Dahlia Avenue? In Silver Lake?"

"Nope. Can't help you."

"I'm sorry. Please excuse the call." I broke the connection. The number Marge gave me had obviously been recycled. Rodney Sullivan was going to require a house call tomorrow.

I dialed Charlie's number. He picked up after two rings, and I briefed him on my conversation with Leslie Anderson. "Moreland said nothing about being on the lot earlier. She said she went to a 24 Hour Fitness Club that morning. I checked with them and couldn't verify her being there. They wouldn't let me see the log of who signed in and out. Nobody seemed to remember her being there because they had a medical emergency. Some old guy apparently had a heart attack."

"What about surveillance cameras?"

"Good point. I didn't look to see if there were any."

"I'll have somebody check it out."

I gave him the club's address and then asked, "Anything else shake loose?"

"We heard from the coroner on Elaine. There was cyanide in the bottle. The stuff can enter the body by inhalation, ingestion, or direct contact with the skin. Apparently it prevents the body's cells from using oxygen. Death is pretty quick. Minutes."

"Okay," I said thickly.

"The body's been released to this Vince Ferraro."

"Okay." I stared at the phone. To say something, I said, "Anything else?"

"Lots of prints from the Weddington trailer. The Burgess kid's are all over the place, of course, along with half the rest of the studio. The medicine bottle was clean except for Weddington's prints. We think it was a substitute. Faster to switch bottles than to switch contents."

"You find any prints for Sam Goldberg?"

"From the knob on the door. He was in the place like he said."

"Nowhere else?"

"Not that we found."

My mind was sluggish. I wanted to hang up and have half a dozen drinks and a nap. I forced a question. "Any news on Murphy?"

"The lab matched the fibers under her fingernails with the fabric of the pillow. Nothing else." I heard him talking to someone in the background. "Somebody's bustin' my chops here, Eddie. I gotta go."

"Right. I'll check with you later."

I broke the connection and stared into space. Cyanide. Fierce, quick, ruthless.

A medicine for somebody you really wanted to kill.

What had Elaine done?

Chapter Twenty-Two

I went back to Elaine's list of phone numbers in the morning. I had six initial sets and six numbers, and between us Mavis had attached six names to them. Some names were definitely good, others were question marks. We had:

JH. Jeremy Hodges. Definite link to Elaine *and* Sam Goldberg.

RS. The number had rung at Vandalia Bond and Casualty, from which I'd obtained the name Rodney Sullivan. Whether Rodney was RS wasn't certain. But the bonding company presented a direct link to Sam.

AC. Alex Chavez. He hadn't sounded like someone from Elaine's socio-economic class. Still . . . a question mark.

DE. The number rang at a post-production house, Deadline Effects. No definite link to Elaine or Sam, but a tenuous one: DE was in the industry. Question mark.

MP. Mavis had tracked the number to a Milt Pappas. The name was familiar but I couldn't place it. A question mark.

TW. The number was listed to a Travis Wormstead. Question mark.

"You noted their addresses?" I asked Mavis.

"I did, where I had addresses. That's everyone but 'TW.' There wasn't one with the phone number." She printed a page with initials, phone numbers, names and five addresses.

I went to the bottom of the list. Dialed the number beside the initials TW.

"Yes?" The woman sounded like she had just gotten out of bed.

"May I speak to Travis Wormstead?"

"Who?"

"Travis Wormstead."

Her voice launched up the register. "Is that you again, you little shit? If you don't stop calling this number, I'm gonna get hold of my nephew. He's damn sure going to come over there and kick your ass!"

"Sorry, ma'am. I'm calling for a Travis Wormstead."

"There's no goddamn Travis Wormwood here. And if—"

I hung up the phone and pulled my hand back like I'd just touched a hot stove.

I dialed Sam Goldberg's office and his assistant Thelma picked up. "Your timing is impeccable, Eddie. I was about to call you. Elaine's funeral is scheduled for Saturday."

"That's what I was calling you about."

"Three o'clock at Forest Lawn, Hollywood Hills. A reception following at the Smoke House. You know? Next to Warner's?"

"I know it well. See you there."

I broke the connection, passed the information to Mavis, who asked, "Do you want me to take care of sending flowers for you?"

"Would you?"

"How do you want them signed? 'Eddie' or 'Collins Investigations'?"

"Make it 'Eddie and Mavis.' That way it's from you too."

Chapter Twenty-Three

Rumor has it that Tom Mix's faithful steed "Tony, the Wonder Horse" is buried in Silver Lake under what used to be the legendary cowboy's studio. The studio, too, is buried under a shopping center. Poor Tony. At least Trigger got to be stuffed.

Driving through, you could see the ethnic and economic mix, gentrified areas, neighborhoods full of artists and bohemians, coffee houses abutting boutiques and bodegas.

Dahlia Avenue had missed out on any upswing. The house I was looking for was two-story, small and rundown. In front sat a battered blue Subaru. On the curb were two mailboxes, the second one with the address and "½" on it. Someone must live in the rear or upstairs.

I climbed steps to a small porch. The windows facing the street were covered with curtains. I pushed a doorbell, heard no response until the door opened and a large woman filled the space. She looked perfect for the *Jerry Springer Show*: tight black Capri pants, a loose tank top, reddish-brown hair styled by an eggbeater. She was pushing the mid-fifties, and they were pushing back and winning.

"Yeah?"

"I'm looking for Rodney Sullivan." I showed her my license.

"What's he done?"

"Nothing, I hope. I'm involved in a case and need to talk to him."

"He used to live here, but he's gone. He rented the place in back. Been gone for a while, though."

"How long?"

"Six, eight mnoths."

"Did you know him well?"

"Well enough to collect the rent."

"Did he leave a forwarding address?"

"Nope."

"Never stopped by to pick up mail?"

"I ain't seen him since he left."

"Do you know where he worked?"

"Not really." She shifted her weight, signaling she was getting tired of being helpful. "All's I know is he paid his rent. Nice fella. Went out every morning wearing a tie. Anything else? I'm kinda busy."

I handed her one of my cards, and she shut the door. I walked over to a driveway that ran alongside the house. A metal gate spanned the paved surface about twenty yards down. I walked back to the gate and saw what appeared to be a renovated garage at the end. Once the home of Rodney Sullivan.

I headed back to the street.

Mavis had done what she could with our names. "Statewide I found a hundred and ninety-seven Rodney Sullivans," she reported. "Forty-one in L.A. down to San Diego."

"I would've thought there'd be more."

"Me too. Not many for Wormstead. Only eight. No Travis, so I printed out anybody with the initial 'T' in front of it. . . . I guess you didn't find Sullivan in Silver Lake? Do you want me to start calling these numbers?"

"I'll wade into them tomorrow. What you can do is make up some phony spiel for why I'm calling."

"Some connection to Vandalia?"

"Right."

She was silent for a moment. "Vandalia owes a former employee money?"

"Hard to beat the tried and true," I said approvingly.

I sat in the car at a 7-Eleven on Sunset and looked up the number for Vince Ferraro. It was a lousy time to call, but Ferraro was the best bet for telling me what had been going on in Elaine's life. The Woodland Hills number rang four times and clicked, as the call was forwarded. Ferraro answered, voice deep and resonant.

I introduced myself. "My condolences on your loss."

"And mine on yours," he said. "Elaine spoke of you from time to time. What can I do for you?"

When I told him, he said, "You caught me on the way to the funeral home. I decided to have a public viewing tomorrow. Do you want to meet me there—Forest Lawn?"

Not really.

"Okay," I said.

And drove to Burbank.

The only sound was faint music. Soft lighting chased away the shadows. Just outside the door of one of the viewing rooms stood a tripod with Elaine's name embossed on a large piece of card stock bordered by a floral pattern. A very short man in a dark suit and a black tie stood by the doorway. I doffed my hat as he walked over to me, hands clasped in front of him. A nametag above his breast pocket identified him as Charles Denton.

"May I help you, sir?"

"I'm looking for Vince Ferraro."

"Of course. Are you family?"

"Not really. I was asked to meet him here."

"Mr. Ferraro is viewing the deceased. Shall I inform him of your presence?"

"Yes, thank you."

He bowed slightly and slowly walked into the viewing room. I stayed where I was, feeling nervous and sick. I didn't want to see her. No way that was going to happen.

I was glancing at a guest book on a pedestal when I heard voices behind me. I turned and saw Vince Ferraro. He came over, hand outstretched. He was my height, broad-shouldered, wearing a black suit. A finely chiseled tan face set off a neatly trimmed gray beard. His dark eyes were red-rimmed.

"Eddie? Good to meet you." I extended my hand and he enveloped it in both of his.

We stood uncomfortably looking at each other. He said, "While I was driving over here, I remembered that Elaine mentioned you had started your own investigation office."

I nodded. "I never thought I'd have this kind of case."

"I can imagine. I never expected—well . . . I've done about all I need to do here. Do you want to get a drink or something?"

"I'd like that."

"Let me just have a word with Denton here." He moved off a couple of paces, then came back. "I'm sorry, Eddie. Would you like to pay your respects? I didn't know whether I should have an open viewing, but I'm . . ." He pinched the bridge of his nose, fighting tears. "Tell you what. I'll finish with Denton and meet you out front."

"Fine," I said. He spoke to the undertaker for a moment, then stepped away. Denton again bowed slightly and gestured to me. Reluctantly, I walked into the viewing room.

Floral arrangements filled the chamber. Next to the casket a small table supported more flowers. There was a chair on either side. Her casket was made of a dark wood polished to a high gloss. I walked up to it and saw her lying inside. My knees started to buckle. I backed up to one of the chairs and sat down heavily. Tears welled up and I bit my lip to try and stop them. It didn't do much good. Several gasps almost took my breath away. I struggled for a minute for composure. Then I got up and stood next to her remains.

The body was draped in a dark burgundy dress. Her hands were clasped over her abdomen. Bracelets on her wrists and two rings on her fingers. A single strand of pearls surrounded her neck. Morticians do wonders, I suppose, but she didn't look natural. Chalk white, her face somewhat puffy. Makeup had been applied, but it looked inappropriate.

I was overwhelmed by the finality of it all. Caused by a hideous act of hate and animosity. Memories washed over me. They were laced with regret and a profound sadness. I placed my hand against her cheek and held it there for a moment. The feeling was unlike anything I had ever experienced. It was a small gesture, but I didn't know what else to do. I pulled a handkerchief from my pocket and walked from the room, nodding to Denton where he stood in the doorway.

Ferraro was outside under the portico. He was on his cell. When he saw me, he finished the call and buttoned his overcoat.

"How long has it been since you'd seen her, Eddie?"

"Couple of years."

"As I said, I don't know if I'm doing the right thing having an open casket viewing, but . . ."

He left the sentence hanging.

"You did the right thing."

He nodded and pulled a handkerchief from his pocket and took a swipe at the corners of his eyes.

"There's a place over on Olive. Michael's. Just a little east of NBC. Sound okay?"

"See you there," I said.

He walked to a Lexus as I donned my hat and coat and crossed the parking lot. Twin pairs of headlights pierced the thickening gloom as we drove away, neither of us knowing how to deal with sorrow.

Chapter Twenty-Four

Vince Ferraro sat across the booth from me destroying his swizzle stick. He kept twisting it until he gave up and dropped it beside his gin and tonic. Michael's was almost empty, dimly lit and quiet.

Ferraro told me he was an architect. He had been in San Diego when he heard about Elaine's death.

"I couldn't believe it yesterday when the police told me it was cyanide poisoning. I mean, Christ! That strike you as being a bit extreme?"

"It does. But someone doesn't think in those terms." I sipped from the glass of bourbon in front of me. "Did Elaine tell you about any problems she was having on the set?"

"Well, obviously that ear infection wasn't exactly making it a joy for her to go to work. It seemed to aggravate things."

"How about the people she was working with?"

Ferraro took a swallow from his glass and thought for a moment. "At times she said she was getting a little irritated by the lack of professionalism on the set."

"From anybody in particular?"

"Seems to me I remember her mentioning somebody named Josiah, or Joseph?"

"Josh? Josh Bauer?"

"That's it. An actor?"

"He's the kid playing opposite her."

"Yeah, that's him. She thought he was pretty wet behind the ears." He grinned and took another sip of gin and tonic. "Matter of fact, over the last couple of years she thought they were all wet behind the ears. Comes from starting out in another era, I guess."

"I know the feeling."

"Did you work with her?"

"That's how we met. Doing an industrial film."

He nodded and we sat for a moment, staring into our drinks. "Did Elaine ever mention a problem with Janet Moreland?"

"Not specifically. But I could sense there might have been some ego problems between the two of them."

"In what way?"

"One day she told me that Moreland had gone to Goldberg about some problem they were having. Elaine thought that was rather petty. She felt it was more appropriate to go to the director." He smiled and shook his head. "Even though she thought he was pretty much of a wuss." He finished off his gin and tonic and picked up the mutilated swizzle stick. "Funny thing is, she got along great with the crew. She said the grips and stagehands were the best judge of her performances. She always appreciated their comments."

The waitress walked up to the booth and Vince pointed at my drink. "Refill?" I nodded and he indicated he'd have another as well. As she walked away Vince's cell phone chirped. He pulled it from a pocket and indicated he had to take the call. It was a short exchange that I ignored, thinking of Elaine lying in the casket.

Ferraro put the phone back in his pocket. "Sorry about that."

"Elaine ever mention a guy named Rodney Sullivan to you?"

"I don't believe so."

"How about an attorney, Jeremy Hodges?"

Ferraro turned his head to the side, his brow furrowed. "That name does sound vaguely familiar. Why would I know it?"

"Hodges told me Elaine had consulted him about the possibility of filing a lawsuit against Sam Goldberg. She ever talk to you about it?"

"Now that you mention it, I remember something about that. Several years ago." He paused and sipped from the drink in front of him. "A friend of hers—an actress—had experienced some sexual harassment."

"From Goldberg?"

"I don't remember."

"Do you recall the name of the actress?"

"No, Elaine said the girl wanted to remain anonymous. Elaine spoke to this Hodges on her behalf. I think she just wanted to sound him out about possible grounds, his fee, things like that."

Hodges had mentioned a contract dispute. Sexual harassment would be a different ballgame.

"Let me ask you something, Vince. Could Elaine have been the 'actress friend'?"

He turned the idea over. "I suppose that's possible. But you knew her as well as I did. She was a pretty gutsy lady. I doubt she'd have let harassment get started in the first place."

"You've got a point. Did she mention anything more about her contact with Hodges?"

"No, she didn't. I don't know if she ever followed up on it."

From the bar, two afternoon imbibers burst into laughter. The sound grated on me. I said, "Had she been getting along with Goldberg lately?"

"As much as was necessary. I've met the guy on a couple of occasions. He's not a bundle of gentility."

"Aptly put."

The waitress brought another round. I raised my glass. "To memories. Were you two married?"

"No, we'd talked about it. We just never got around to it. Things seemed pretty comfortable the way they were."

He drank from his glass, then set it down and looked at nothing.

"Gonna be difficult saying goodbye to her," Vince said.

I drove home playing with scenarios of Sam Goldberg demanding sexual favors—and those worked well enough, but when I tried to fit Elaine into the script it fell apart. She might have broken his arm, but I couldn't picture her as a victim, compliant or otherwise.

Parking at my building is never easy. Tonight the single light bulb in the carport ceiling was out. I crept into the spot beside Lenny's Volkswagen, climbed out and barely glimpsed the fast-moving figure that had come from behind the cars. He was swinging something, and I raised my arm but it was too late. A blow slammed the back of my neck. It knocked me against my car's side window. My nose hit the glass and came away dripping blood. I slid along the side of the car, tried to get my feet under me. The club dug into my belly. I doubled over and grabbed him round the waist. More blows pounded my back as I wrestled him out into the alley behind the car.

My feet slipped, my knees cracked on the pavement, and the club hammered my shoulder. I sank down and tried to crawl away. He held both ends of the club and pressed it against my windpipe. Lights flashed behind my eyelids.

Then suddenly I heard a shout.

There was a scuffle behind me. The choker let up. Footsteps ran off, others pursued. I collapsed.

"Eddie, are you all right?"

I looked up into the face of Lenny Daye.

Was I all right? "Yeah, I think so."

I tried to get up, groaned in pain, and he tucked a shoulder under my left arm and helped me hobble to the rear of my car, where I sat on the bumper. My legs felt like heavy Jello.

"Good God, you're leaking. Put your head back." He pulled a handkerchief from his pocket and stuck it under my nose. I packed the nostrils.

"Where the hell did you come from?" I mumbled.

"I was on my way out. Opened the door and saw this asshole straddling you. Do you need a doctor?"

I was woozy and wobbly. "Just give me a couple of minutes."

Lenny retrieved my hat and handed it to me. One of us had stomped on it. He picked up a length of two-by-four and waved it. "This is what he was using. Look at the nails! You're lucky you weren't stabbed."

"One of them caught me." The heel of my left hand was bleeding.

"You're going to need a tetanus shot. Have you got some hydrogen peroxide?"

"I think so."

Lenny looked at the carport ceiling. "The damn bulb has been smashed. Who the hell was that?"

"Don't have a clue. Did you get a look at him?"

"A little. You know any redheads?"

"I know one," I said.

Chapter Twenty-Five

Rodney Sullivan.

Besides Marge at Vandalia Bond, the only person who knew I was looking for Sullivan was the woman at the Dahlia Avenue address. I'd given her my card that had the office address. She'd passed it along to Sullivan.

Lenny Daye had helped me upstairs and cleaned the nail wound with hydrogen peroxide. Ice cubes, Ibuprofen and bourbon took my mind off assorted discomforts. Even so I didn't sleep worth a damn.

Mavis arrived early, saw the boss with a bandaged hand, a partly black eye, a swollen nose and an ice bag on his shoulder. "Should I ask?" she said.

"I wouldn't."

But she did anyway, and I gave her a recap from last night while she searched the Dahlia Avenue address. The occupant's name was Shirley Jackson. I left Mavis to cold call the names on our printout.

I drove to Silver Lake, stopped a few numbers down on Dahlia Avenue. A letter carrier pushed a little three-wheeled cart down the street. She stopped at Shirley Jackson's house and deposited envelopes in both mailboxes. I waited until she was off the block, then went up and had a look. Shirley Jackson and Francine Bailey had mail. Nothing for Rodney Sullivan.

No one answered the doorbell. I hit it again and looked through a window. No movement. The living room was strewn with clutter: newspapers piled on a coffee table, sofa covered with a ratty blanket, a TV screen that was dark.

I leaned on the doorbell once more for good measure and waited. She could have seen me coming and felt we'd talked enough.

I went down the driveway, opened the metal gate. Weeds grew from the pavement. A rusty barbecue grill sat in the middle of the backyard, under a clothesline suspended from a broken-down porch to a withered tree.

What used to be the garage doors were now French windows. Around to the side was a single door. I knocked and an elderly woman's head appeared.

"Francine Bailey?"

"You from the Water Department?"

"No, ma'am. I'm looking for Shirley Jackson."

"She lives in the front house."

"I know. Would you by any chance know where she is?"

She dropped her chin to look at me through strands of gray hair. "She ain't paid her bill either?"

"I wouldn't know, ma'am."

"Mine's late, I know. I told you people over the phone I'd pay you a little bit at a time."

"I'm not from the Water Department, ma'am. A fellow used to live here by the name of Rodney Sullivan. Do you know who he is?"

"Nope. Don't think so."

"A redheaded guy? Maybe he came by here to pick up some mail or something?"

She scratched her nose with my card. "I mighta seen him one day."

"Do you remember when?"

"Awhile back. I think he was from the Water Department."

I thanked her, started for the street and then diverted to the rickety back porch. When I knocked, the screen door rattled in its frame. That was all that happened. Two more attempts didn't rouse anyone. There was a tarp covering something in a corner, a tall bundle wrapped with a bungee cord that held down a piece of paper. On the paper the name "Rodney" was scrawled in pencil.

I lifted a corner of the tarp, saw an easy chair with a box filling the seat.

Shirley Jackson was definitely a fibber.

By the time I got back to my office Mavis had made a dozen calls to Rodney Sullivans. Her spiel mentioning Vandalia Bond and Casualty had yielded no takers.

Chapter Twenty-Six

It felt like the third act of Thornton Wilder's classic play *Our Town*. At least a dozen black umbrellas were clustered around Elaine's casket, as if she were playing Emily Webb and the entire town of Grover's Corners was standing in the rain at her funeral.

I'm not particularly good with these affairs. Nor is anyone I suppose. There's something about the ritual, the rigidity of the proceedings that has always baffled me. The preponderance of black. The stoic men of the cloth, standing in front of a group of people they don't know, extolling the virtues of someone else they didn't know.

I listened to the rain spattering my umbrella. Somehow I had the feeling that Elaine would rather have had everyone sitting around her ashes getting sloppy drunk, regaling one other with bawdy stories and fond memories.

However, that wasn't my decision. Hank Schultz, her brother, had flown in from Miles City, Montana and had worked on the arrangements with Vince Ferraro. Hank and I had met before. He sold farm implements. He didn't know much about "the acting game." I didn't know much about three-bottom plows, so our conversation went nowhere. He was a pleasant enough guy. Now he stood next to Vince Ferraro and Sam Goldberg, glancing at the mourners from time to time, his expression openly curious. The *Flames of Desire* company was well represented. I couldn't refrain from wondering if Elaine's murderer was among them. I caught Sam Goldberg dabbing at his eyes with a handkerchief. Were they real tears? Janet Moreland and Madeline Schmidt were both appropriately garbed in black. Janet had gone so far as to wear a small hat with a veil draping her face. Two bereaved women mourning the loss of a colleague? Janet had already been caught in an apparent lie regarding her whereabouts that day.

The minister's words ended and the mourners started filing back to their cars. I stood looking at the casket. Ferraro was on the other side. After a moment I moved over to him, shook his hand and walked off. His grief was more immediate than mine.

"Are you okay, Eddie?" Mavis asked. She walked next to me, tightly clasping my arm. "It was a nice service."

I agreed it was. We caught up with Thelma and Sam. The smoke from his freshly lit cigar hung in the thick humidity. He stuck out a hand. I took it as he said, "She'll be missed, m'boy."

Thelma gave me a hug and a little pat on the cheek. She didn't say anything. I shook the rain from my umbrella and spotted Janet and Madeline walking toward a black Range Rover. I excused myself and started after them.

"Miss Moreland?" I called. Both women turned.

"Hello, Mr. Collins," Janet said. She extended a black-gloved hand. "Mr. Goldberg told me you and Elaine had been married. I didn't realize. My condolences on your loss."

"Thank you."

"Please know that you're in my prayers." I nodded. She turned to Madeline. "You remember Madeline, of course."

"My goodness, Mr. Collins," Madeline said, "what happened to your eye?"

"Little run-in with a car door. After we spoke the other day, I thought of something else I need to ask you."

"Right now?" Janet's eyebrows arched in surprise. "After such a sad occasion?"

"It'll save me another trip to the lot."

"Yes, of course. Had you planned on coming over to the reception?"

"Yes."

"Why don't we meet there?"

"Fine. A couple of minutes is all I need."

"Absolutely."

I nodded and the two women headed for the Range Rover. A furtive, whispered conversation passed between them. If I were handicapping it, I'd have said Madeline disputed and Janet prevailed.

Off in the distance I could see a backhoe already at work, pushing a mound of earth onto Elaine's casket.

The reception consisted of dinner at the Smoke House, a Burbank landmark known for its garlic bread. Elaine, who appreciated surreal California moments, must have been laughing her ass off.

A couple of stiff drinks let me stifle curmudgeonly thoughts. The ritual Meal was probably a good thing. It brought people together, and tonight it turned into a celebration of Elaine's life. She would have approved. I was sorry that Mavis, who had begged off and gone home, missed it.

Janet Moreland caught my eye at one point and the two women and I converged on an empty table. Janet placed a small black purse next to her coffee cup. She had removed her black hat. "Did you and Elaine ever work together, Mr. Collins?"

"Eddie," I said. "Just once. We met doing an industrial film."

"I've done a few of those myself. Impossible things to memorize, aren't they?"

"They're killers."

"And forget about applying any acting techniques," Madeline chimed in. "A student of mine once came to me for help with one of those things. I threw up my hands and waved the white flag." She smiled and shook her head.

"You said you had something to ask, Eddie?" Janet said.

"I understand Betty Murphy saw you on the Americana lot early in the morning the day of the murder. Is that correct?"

Two young women who apparently were part of the movie's production staff walked by and offered their greetings to Moreland, who smiled at them and then told me, "I had intended to call you after we spoke, but I seemed to have misplaced your card. Betty was correct. I forgot to tell you that I briefly came on the lot before my call."

"Why was that?"

"I had left my script in my trailer. I needed it before Madeline and I could do our dialogue work that morning. When I came back later and learned what had happened, I was just devastated. With all the confusion around the lot it completely slipped my mind."

"Did you get the script before you went to the 24 Hour Fitness Club?"

"No. After."

"I stopped in at the club but they don't seem to recall you being there."

"Really? That's strange. I confess I don't normally chit-chat with people a lot. Just do my workout and leave. But I'm on a first-name basis with most of the staff."

I thought she was lying.

"Thanks for your time, ladies," I said as I rose from the table.

"Again, our condolences on your loss, Eddie," Janet said.

"And take care of that eye," Madeline added.

Elaine's brother, Hank Schultz, sat by himself in a corner with a glass of beer. He looked as out of place as a homeless man in Beverly Hills. I pulled a chair out and sat across from him.

He gestured to my eye and said, "How'd the other guy look?"

"He took off before I had a chance to find out." We laughed and sipped our drinks.

"How you doin', Hank?"

"Pretty good. Glad it's over. Can't wait to get out of here."

"L.A. getting to you?"

"Give me land, lots of land, as my daddy used to say."

"You going back tonight?"

"Eleven-thirty. Red eye, I guess they call it. Through Salt Lake."

"Need a lift to the airport?"

"Naw, Mr. Ferraro has got it all figured out. One of those limo jobbies. Good Lord, don't that make me feel foolish? Sittin' in the back there all by myself. Almost as much room as my tool shed." He looked across the room as a bubble of laughter erupted from the Hollywood types. "Sounds like they're havin' a good time."

"They're probably telling stories about Elaine. She had a lot of friends in the business."

"Tell me something, Eddie. Are they as phony as they look?"

I grinned and took a pull off my drink. "Well, Hank, some of them are. Sometimes, anyway."

He looked at me, sadness filling his eyes. "I know it's been awhile since you two split up, but did you see much of Elaine?"

"We ran into each other from time to time. Why?"

"I'm tryin' to figure out why in the hell somebody would do something like that to her." He clenched his jaw and blinked back the tears that began to well up in his eyes.

"I'm going to do my damnedest to find out, Hank." My words were small comfort to either of us.

Hank finished his beer and I looked up to see Vince Ferraro coming to the table. Behind him Sam Goldberg walked toward the bar. Vince straddled a chair and said, "Why don't you come over to the table, Hank, and meet everyone? We're remembering some of the good times we had with Elaine. I'm sure they'd love to hear some of yours." He put a hand on Hank's shoulder and turned to me. "You too, Eddie."

"Thanks, Vince, but I'm going to cash it in. I've got to talk to Sam about something."

I shook hands with Hank, and the handshake turned into a hug. I clapped him on one shoulder. "Take care of yourself," I said. "Give my best to the family."

Sam was perched on a stool at the bar, watching a hockey game on TV. As I sat next to him, he signaled the bartender.

"Another one for me and one for the young fella here." I asked for a double Maker's Mark and pulled a dish of peanuts in front of me.

"Oh, hell yes, the most expensive stuff," Sam said. He chuckled.

"Don't want to disappoint you, Sam."

We raised our glasses. "To Elaine," he said.

I echoed his toast and we drank.

Sam said, "Look, I shot my mouth off the other night. I was out of line."

"Forget it, Sam."

"The cops gotta do their thing. I know that. Tell that lieutenant it won't happen again."

I pushed the peanuts dish in his direction but he shook his head.

"That tooth still bothering you?"

"Drivin' me nuts." A shout erupted from the other end of the bar. I looked up to see a replay of someone scoring a goal. "What's going on with the investigation? Any leads?"

"LAPD hasn't made much progress. They can't put anybody at the crime scenes. Too many people roaming around."

"What about your end of it? Find out anything?"

"Maybe a couple of things." I nibbled a few peanuts and debated whether this was the right time to ask him about Elaine's dealings with Jeremy Hodges. It had to be done sooner or later. "You know a lawyer named Jeremy Hodges?"

Sam looked down at the bar. "Nope. Who is he? Some schmuck that's gonna sue me or something?"

"He said he invested money in your pictures."

"He might have. I don't know. I'd have to look. How the hell did you dig him up?"

"Following up a lead. He told me Elaine had talked to him about maybe filing a lawsuit against you. Something about a contract dispute?"

Sam froze with his glass halfway to his mouth and turned to look at me, his eyes narrowing.

"What was that all about?" I asked.

He set his drink on the bar and swiveled to face me. "Now, just a minute. Just a goddamn minute. First, some asshole cop starts busting my chops about a bottle of toothache medicine I happen to have in my office. Now you're sitting here asking me about some old stupid-ass disagreement I had with someone that's just been killed. I didn't fall off a turnip truck yesterday. If you think you can pin some fucking motive on me in this thing, you're barking up the wrong goddamn tree."

"I'm only trying—"

"You're only trying to implicate me in this mess. It's damn sure not going to work. Why in the hell would I want to kill Elaine, for crissakes? Her name on one of my pictures made it a gold mine. I treated her like a princess. This is bullshit, Eddie!"

"I'm not making accusations. I'm trying to find out what was going on in her life, Sam. If anybody had a grudge against her."

"I had no fuckin' grudge. We got along fine."

"Why did she talk to Hodges about suing you?"

"Oh, for crissakes, we had a little beef over one of her contracts. She accused me of holding back money from her. Some misunderstanding about net and gross points. We worked it out."

"And that was it?"

"That was it."

"She never brought it up again?"

"Never. Water under the goddamn bridge."

Sam signaled the bartender. "You ready?"

I got the next round and cleared out.

One of the names from Elaine's phone list had finally clicked. Milt Pappas had an address in Bel Air. Time to see if he knew who Jeremy Hodges was.

Chapter Twenty-Seven

With all the traffic in Los Angeles, tailing someone is easy. You just blend in, go with the flow. At night headlights make the job a little more obvious. Someone behind me was being obvious. Until Rodney Sullivan's visit, I probably wouldn't have noticed, or would have dismissed the steady presence as another driver headed from Burbank to Bel Air. Now I was watching the rear view mirror.

The headlights had followed me all the way down Cahuenga. They were about fifty yards behind me as I headed west on Franklin. I hung an abrupt left on Camino, pulled to a curb and doused the lights. The other vehicle continued down Franklin. So maybe I was a little paranoid. Maybe not.

I got back on the road and looked for other cars that liked me too much. None seemed to.

Milt Pappas. The memory of him was vague, but it was there. He had hosted a soiree at his home after a screening of one of Elaine's pictures. I had tagged along, despite not wanting to schmooze and be regarded as Mr. Elaine Weddington. The film met with indifference. The party, however, was a hit. The tab for the food and liquor could have funded a small third-world revolution.

After an hour I choked on empty talk. Air-kisses were flitting around the spacious house like mosquitoes looking for lunch. I walked through a set of French doors, found a shimmering pool, and retreated toward a little pool house nestled under a magnolia tree.

Noise came from the pool house. I looked inside. Milt Pappas was lying on a bench, his trousers around his ankles. Straddling him, panting like she was in training, was the young woman who had played Elaine's younger sister in the new film. Lori Talmadge was her name. She had gone on to work quite a bit, although I hadn't heard much about her lately. She saw me standing in the doorway and put her finger to her lips. She flashed a big grin as she settled in for the home stretch.

I remembered that moment better than I remembered Milt Pappas's face.

The front of the house hadn't changed. The entrance gate was flanked by two miniature oil derricks, draped in small lights that made them look like Christmas trees. Parked in the driveway was a red Honda with a Domino's Pizza sign attached to the top.

I parked across the street. When the Honda came down the driveway and the gate opened, I waved to the pizza man and walked in.

An Hispanic woman in a crisp uniform answered the bell and went to announce me.

Pappas filled in the blank spots in my memory. He was ample in the waistline, round-faced, sparse on top: a guy who won't concede to baldness but keeps dropping the part farther toward the ear and combing the few remaining strands over the pate until he looks like someone has doodled on him with a Magic Marker. He held a dinner napkin in one hand.

"Can I help you?"

I handed him one of my cards. "Name's Eddie Collins. I'm investigating the murder of Elaine Weddington."

"Who?"

"The actress Elaine Weddington. A few years back you hosted a party here after a screening of one of her pictures."

He thought for a moment. "Oh, yeah, right. I invested a few bucks in it. Can't remember the name of the piece of shit. I lost my shirt."

There it was. A link with Jeremy Hodges. Now I had to see if it went any further.

Milt wiped his mouth with the napkin and tossed it on a foyer table, knocking over a small family picture. He put his chubby little paws on his love handles and started swabbing the inside of his mouth with his tongue. "How'd you find this place?"

"I copped an invitation to that party."

"That right? Well, what do you want?"

"A list of names turned up at the murder scene. Yours was on it."

"So?"

"Why would your name and phone number be found at the scene of a murder?"

"How the hell should I know?"

"There's a lawyer out in Century City who's also on the list. He told me he invested in one of Goldberg's pictures too. In return he got to spend some time with Weddington. Anything like that happen with you, Milt?"

He stared at me for a long moment. His dark eyes bored a hole in me. Suddenly his mitts came off the love handles and one of them jabbed the air. "I think it's time for you to leave, pal."

I stood my ground. "Did you ever put a lock on that pool house of yours?"

"What the fuck you talking about?"

"When I was here at the party, I stuck my head in your pool house and saw a young actress named Lori Talmadge squatted over you. I wonder if the Missus knows who Lori Talmadge is."

"Hey!" He grabbed my arm, then let it go. He took a few steps to a heavy oak door, slid it open. "In here."

I followed him into a room that was dark and lined with shelves of books. Pappas went to a heavy desk, poured himself a brandy. He tossed back a mouthful and turned to me. "All right, what the fuck is this all about?"

"Hell of a chill out there, Milt. A good brandy would probably cut it."

He shook his head and poured me a drink. "What do you want?"

"Did you ever receive any . . . I guess you'd call them 'favors' from Elaine Weddington? You know, kick some money into a movie, meet the star? Something like that?"

"Yeah, I met her a couple of times."

"In what context?"

"What do you mean?"

"What did you do? Dinner? Drinks? Sex?"

He set his brandy on the desk. "I outta knock you on your ass, Collins. What the fuck kind of question is that?"

"A straight one."

"If you spill a word of this, Collins, I'll sue you for every fuckin' nickel you have. After I find you and kick the shit out of you."

"Our little secret, Milt."

He ran his hand across the top of his head, mussing the doodle marks. "Some guy told me about something called 'Sleep With a Star'. I'd give him a check and my phone number."

"Who was the guy?"

"Hicks was his name. Joey Hicks. I called him and he always got back to me with a meeting place."

"How many women?"

"I don't know."

"Weddington was one of them?"

"Yeah. I got together with her a couple of times."

"How long ago?"

"Aw, shit, years . . ."

"I still don't get why your name should be on this list."

"Beats the hell out of me."

"Weddington wouldn't have been blackmailing you, would she?"

"What for?"

"Think about it, Milt."

He did. "Naw, I never heard anything from her. Look, Collins, she was a nice lady. I enjoyed her company. That's all it was. I'm sorry to hear she was murdered. But I didn't have a damn thing to do with it."

"Do the names Jeremy Hodges and Rodney Sullivan mean anything to you?"

"Never heard of 'em." He began thinking about the brandy again.

"Where do I find Joey Hicks?"

"Last I knew he managed a little bar called the Cricket Lounge. It's in one of the hotels on the Strip. I forget which one."

Chapter Twenty-Eight

Before getting into the car I opened the trunk and took my Beretta 21 Bobcat from its locked box. I seldom carry it and I didn't think I was going to shoot anyone. But if my red-headed mugger showed up I might reconsider.

Prostitution.

Milt Pappas had defined it: money for the opportunity of meeting Elaine. Jeremy Hodges had put the suspicion in my head. Pappas confirmed it.

But why? I couldn't believe that the strong-minded woman who had shared my life had gone down this path without being coerced. Anger gnawed at me.

Behind me some fool figured the mist on the highway meant he had to blind me with his high beams. Rodney Sullivan? I hit Sunset and turned east, flicking the mirror to a different angle. The vehicle followed.

The Cricket Lounge was familiar to me. I didn't know if it still existed, but I spotted the hotel and found a parking place on a side street. Traffic continued on Sunset. None of it looked suspicious. I dropped the Beretta into the pocket of my coat and walked to the lobby.

A bored desk clerk gave me half a look. Two bearded, elderly gentlemen in rumpled suits sprawled on a beige sofa under a potted palm. Live music came from a doorway under a neon sign shaped like an insect. The place hadn't changed.

The lounge was dimly lit. Tables and several booths splayed out in front of a slightly raised platform where a jazz trio was playing. A small bar was to my left. A tall redheaded woman presided behind it. Another woman, this one young and blond, carried a tray of drinks to a couple seated in a corner.

I took a table by the door. The waitress arrived with a smile.

"Good evening, sir. What'll it be?"

"Double Jim Beam, neat. What's on tap?"

"Amstel, Michelob dark and Coors."

"Amstel'll do it."

The jazz trio was good, unobtrusive. An older black guy on the bull fiddle fingered his way through a nice riff.

The waitress returned and made change from a twenty. I handed her a five. She tapped the table with her knuckles. "Thank you, sir."

"Does Joey Hicks still manage this place?"

"Sure does."

"He around?"

"He's due at nine."

"Thanks." My watch said eight-fifteen. I settled in to wait. The music was good company.

Nine o'clock arrived, along with a new waitress. She was brunette and somewhat older than the first one. She came up to my table and I ordered another round. The piano player yielded to a young man on an alto sax, who sidled into a somber moody segment.

At ten after nine, three men burst through the door. They were boisterous and looked like they'd brought the party from somewhere else. They jostled their way to the bar. The shortest one went around behind. That had to be Hicks.

He took off his coat, exposing a light blue shirt that shimmered like silk. He wore pleated black slacks. Chains hung from his neck, rings and bracelets decorated his hands and wrists. His black hair was swept up in a pompadour that rivaled Elvis. A small moustache grew on his upper lip. A bit of a soul patch sprouted beneath his lower lip.

I watched him, seething. He set drinks in front of his friends. They bantered with the waitress. After a few minutes, Hicks headed down a hallway beside the bar. It was now or never.

I followed him. The restrooms flanked one another. A payphone was bolted to one wall.

I pushed the door open and saw Hicks at one of two urinals. The cramped room had one stall. The floor was covered with cracked tiles. Two sinks and air dryers occupied the wall to my left. A chair sat in the nearest corner. I splashed water on my hands in a sink. While the dryer ran, Hicks flushed the urinal and stuck his hands under the second faucet.

"How's it goin'?" I said. I walked to the corner and picked up the chair. His eyes followed me.

"Can't complain," he replied.

I propped the chair under the doorknob. The rear legs caught on the cracks in the tile. "You Joey Hicks?"

"Yeah, man. Who're you? And what the fuck you doin'?"

"I'm a friend of Milt Pappas." I stuffed my hands in my pockets. One of them wrapped around the Beretta.

The faucet stopped and Hicks turned to me.

"That supposed to mean something to me?"

"How about Jeremy Hodges?"

"Hey, Dude, I don't know what the fuck you're talkin' about. And put the damn chair back." He punched the dryer and stuck his hands under the flow of hot air.

I grabbed him by the front of his silk shirt with my left hand and shoved him through the door of the stall and up against the wall. His head connected with the tile. He straddled the commode. I pulled the gun from my pocket and stuck the barrel against the little patch of whiskers under his mouth. His eyes widened as he struggled to regain his footing.

"What the fuck?" He grabbed the back of his head.

"Milt Pappas says he did business with you."

"I don't know no fucking Milt."

"Come on, Joey. You used to run a string of call girls. It was called 'Sleep With a Star.' Elaine Weddington was one of the girls. That name ring a bell?"

"Man, I don't know what the hell you're talkin' about! Put the fuckin' gun away!"

I cocked the Beretta and pushed it against his soul patch. "Did you run the girls, Joey?"

His eyes darted side to side. "That was a long time ago. And it wasn't me. I was only working for somebody."

"Who?"

"He's gonna kill me, man!"

"Who were you working for, Joey?" I pushed the gun harder.

"Okay, okay. Jesus Christ!" I relaxed my hold on his shirt front. He slid down and collapsed on the stool. One of his hands hit the flush handle. The water started running and he looked cross-eyed up along the barrel of the gun into my eyes.

"The dude's name was Goldberg. Sam Goldberg."

My first instinct was to show up on Sam's doorstep and see if I could refrain from killing him.

Bad idea unless I found I couldn't resist. If I merely confronted Sam, he would deny everything. If I kicked his ass but didn't kill him, he would ban me from the lot, probably press charges—though he might want to avoid cops; if I had gotten the story out of Pappas and Hicks, so could the police. But nothing I had—and nothing I could see the police getting—would tie the call girl ring to Elaine's death.

Jeremy Hodges, Milt Pappas and Joey Hicks had all said their involvement with Elaine had been in the past. How long ago? Why had she stopped—if she had? Had she blackmailed Hodges or Pappas? Regardless of the answer to that, whoever poisoned her almost had to have been on the *Flames of Desire* lot. Who in that group had known Elaine long enough to have been part of her past?

The questions took me in a circle, because I knew the answer.

Sam Goldberg.

Sam Goldberg had known her since she arrived in Hollywood.

I drove a while, found a liquor store, decided a pint of bourbon might help my thinking. I went in and bought one, came out into a side parking lot and opened the front door of my car.

The ceiling light came on. I gathered my coat around me to get in.

That's when I heard the shot.

Something plowed into my upper right arm. The jolt slammed me against the open car door. I started to crumple. My head hit the corner of the door.

After that, I wasn't around.

Chapter Twenty-Nine

A young Asian man leaned over my shoulder. He was tearing adhesive tape off my upper arm. It hurt and I winced. I was in bed under acoustic tile and a sprinkler head. Otherwise there was nothing to look at. "Ah, Mr. Collins," the tape puller said. "Welcome back. How do you feel?"

"Like I've done ten rounds with Mike Tyson. Who are you and where am I?" The words croaked. My throat felt like sandpaper.

"I'm Mr. Han. You're in Cedars Sinai. Do you need some water?"

Mavis appeared, handed me a glass of water with a flexible straw in it. I drank eagerly. Fritz, her husband, the bus driver, walked up behind her.

"Hey, how you doin', Hoss?" he said.

"What are you doing here? The bus company fire you?"

"Nope. It's Sunday."

"Really?" The cobwebs began to dissolve in my head. I found it hard to believe that the miseries of Elaine's funeral, Milt Pappas and Joey Hicks had occurred only yesterday.

"Fritz brought me over," Mavis said. She took the glass from me and filled it from a pitcher on a cluttered table next to the bed. She handed it back. "He said he wanted to see you, too. Isn't that nice?"

"He's a pussycat." I shook the hand he extended. It was his left, considerate soul that he is.

"Sam Goldberg called and he said he wants to see you as soon as he can."

The mention of the man's name caused my right arm to suddenly start aching again. I put the straw to my lips and slurped. Mavis started in on a mother-hen routine, straightening linens and tossing things into a wastepaper basket at her feet.

"Can somebody tell me what happened?" I asked.

"You were shot," Mavis said.

"How did I get here?"

"You were brought in about ten-thirty last evening," Han said. He punctuated his remark with a final yank of tape. I remembered a flash of a pickup truck careening along the street.

"Some kids," I said. "In a red pickup. I think one of them did it."

"Think again," Fritz said. "They were the ones who called the ambulance."

"They saw the interior light on in your car and you on the ground, Eddie," Mavis said. "They stayed there with you until it came. You were out cold and bleeding all over the place."

"Kid's name was Alejandro Sanchez," Fritz said. "Told the paramedics he wanted to know how you came out."

"Isn't that something?" Mavis said.

"Yeah," I muttered. Han began applying a new bandage to my arm.

"How bad is it?" I asked him.

"Your doctor will tell you specifically. Nothing vital was injured. You did lose some blood, and you've got a nasty cut on your forehead."

I became aware of the bandage over my left eye. I remembered hitting the door as I fell. I asked Mavis, "How did you know I was here?"

"They found your cards in your wallet," she replied. "I got the message the hospital left at the office when I called to apologize for ducking the reception."

A tall man came into the room. "I'm Doctor Eckstein. How are you feeling, Mr. Collins?"

"I've been better."

He nodded and turned to Han, who had finished the bandage. "How does it look?"

"No sign of infection."

The doc consulted the chart in front of him. "You caught a little bit of luck last night. Are you a southpaw?"

"Nope."

"In that case, you might have a little difficulty doing some routine movements. I'll give you something for the pain. The muscle should heal just fine. By the way, we had to file a police report."

His eyebrow may have lifted a fraction, but probably not. Information delivered, he was gone. Mr. Han followed, and pretty soon Mavis ran out of things to straighten up and took her husband home.

In the morning I was hoping to get cut loose before visitors showed up. I didn't want to see the cops. And I didn't want to see Sam Goldberg. Mavis had ordered the hospital to call her when it was time to pick me up. She arrived half a second ahead of Goldberg.

He carried a bouquet of flowers, which he automatically handed to Mavis. He looked down at me. "What the hell happened? I thought you were going home after the Smoke House?"

I hated the sight of him. Hated having to pretend. "I took a detour."

"You all right?"

"Yeah, about to go home."

"I'll stop in the office on my way out and tell them to send the bill to me."

"I've got insurance, Sam."

"I know you got insurance. It sure as hell ain't gonna pick up everything. You let me worry about it."

I watched his friendly, confident face, trying to glean any hint that the term "pimp" didn't apply to him. I couldn't. I had learned too much.

"I was going to bring you a bottle of bourbon, but the wife didn't think that was a good idea. So I got you some flowers. I don't know if they're the right kind. What the hell do I know about flowers? Flowers are flowers, right?" He turned to Mavis. "What do you think?"

"They're lovely, Sam. They'll look good in the office."

Sam studied my bandage as if he didn't hear her. "So, somebody winged you, huh?"

I nodded.

"Any idea who it was?"

"Haven't got a clue."

"Hurts like hell, I bet."

"Pretty sore, yeah."

"You get your busted wing fixed. Can't have you walking around like a goddamn cripple, for crissakes. You wanna use the cabin up at Big Bear?"

"No thanks."

"You're welcome to it. I hate the damn place. Can't stand the smell of those fucking pine trees." He turned to Mavis and said as an afterthought, "Pardon my French . . . uh . . . Marla, isn't it?"

"Mavis." She forced herself to smile. I knew she was probably ready to feed him his flowers.

"Right," he said. He came closer to the bed. "Listen, Eddie, no hard feelings about what we discussed the other night, okay?"

"No hard feelings, Sam."

"If there's anything you need, don't hesitate to give me a call. You got it?"

"I got it."

"All right, then. I gotta go. We're still tryin' to figure out how the hell to make a movie." He started for the door and stopped in front of Mavis. "You're getting better lookin' every time I see you. Why don't you come and work for me?"

"Not a chance."

"That's what he says too. I keep tellin' him he's a damn fool." He let loose a throaty chuckle. "Fuckin' guy won't listen to me."

I filled Mavis in on my encounters with Pappas and Hicks.

"And you didn't see who shot you?"

"No."

"It could have been Sam?"

"Or Rodney Sullivan. Or Pappas or Hicks—hell, or Janet Moreland. There's no shortage of liars I've run into."

She threw Sam's flowers in the wastepaper basket. "You aren't going to confront Sam?"

"He'd just deny it."

"You can go to the cops."

"Then I'd have to drag Elaine's name through it. Without having proof of anything."

"Come on," she said, "I'll give you a ride home."

Chapter Thirty

"Let's take a detour," I said. "Up to Sunset and head east."

She was driving her big white pickup, which spent most of its time in the repair shop eating Mavis's salary. Driving it let her think she was the meanest thing on the road.

I told her about the pile of Rodney Sullivan's furniture on his former landlady's back porch. We turned onto Dahlia and she pulled to the curb. A light blue Subaru sat in front of Shirley Jackson's house. "I think that's her car," I said.

I reached across with my left hand and opened the truck's door. Over my shoulder I saw Mavis getting out.

"Where you going?"

"You need backup."

"I don't need backup."

"Tell that to our neighbor Lenny after he pulled Sullivan off you."

"Sullivan was waiting for me. Besides, this is a woman we're dealing with."

"Probably more than a match for you," she said, and started toward the house. I double-timed to catch up, right arm bouncing in its sling against my chest.

I rang the doorbell, waited, and punched it again. Finally the door opened a crack and Shirley Jackson peeked out.

"Remember me?"

"The private eye." Her eyes shifted to Mavis. "Who's she?"

Mavis said, "I'm the muscle."

"Where's Rodney Sullivan?" I said.

"I told you I don't know."

"Not good enough. After I gave you my card the other day, he tried to kill me."

"That's too bad. But I still don't know where he is."

"Cut the crap. You gave him my name and address."

"You better get the hell off my porch before I call the cops."

She started to push the door shut. Before I could get my foot in the opening Mavis shouldered herself into the house. Jackson stumbled backwards, let out a screech.

Mavis grabbed the front of her yellow terry-cloth robe. "If my boss gets killed, I'm out of a job. I need the work. Now where's Sullivan?"

Jackson backed up to a table and turned to grab a phone. Mavis twisted it away from her. "If you call the cops, lady, they're going to find out you're harboring a criminal." She tapped her on the chest with the receiver. "Here you go if you want."

"Get her the hell away from me."

I said, "There's a pile of furniture on your back porch with Sullivan's name on it. He leave it to you in his will?"

Jackson ran a wrinkled hand through her hair. "All right, he called me. I told him I'd hang onto the furniture until he found a place to live. He called me after you were here and said he'd found a condo."

"Where?"

"I don't know. He didn't tell me."

"He leave his phone number?"

"No."

"How'd he get my address?"

"How the hell should I know? You're in the Yellow Pages, aren't you?" She sank down onto a sofa, dug a package of cigarettes from her robe. "Look, I swear to God I don't know where he is. When he called I thought he should know somebody's looking for him. That's all."

Mavis stepped close to her. "Why would he want to kill Mr. Collins? Did Sullivan say he knew him?"

"No." Jackson lit a cigarette, coughed out smoke.

"Did Sullivan ever mention the name Elaine Weddington?" I said.

"That movie star that was killed?"

"That's the one."

"Nah, he never mentioned her."

"Sullivan jumped me and damn near killed me," I said. "Then I think he took a shot at me. He found me because of you. You might want to think about that."

She didn't answer.

I stared at her. "Get his phone number the next time he calls."

"Yeah, yeah, all right."

There was about as much chance of that happening as me showing up on "Dancing With the Stars."

We split up the lists of Travis Wormstead and Rodney Sullivan phone numbers. I didn't make any progress. A guy who thought I might be recruiting for the IRA was the highlight of the afternoon. Mavis fared no better.

"What if Sullivan called Jackson from a cell phone?" I said. "How would someone get his number?"

She found a cell phone directory on the net. "To get specifics, like the address, you have to pay them money. You want to?"

"What do you think?"

"Well, if we can't find Sullivan on a land line search, chances are he'll be unlisted with cell phone directories too."

"Yeah, good point." I sank into a chair in front of her desk.

"You don't look too good, Eddie. You should lie down."

"I think you're right."

She followed me into my office, and I gave her my list of numbers.

Chapter Thirty-One

Banging on the wall woke me up. My watch told me I'd been asleep for little over an hour.

"Eddie? Lieutenant Rivers is here."

I pulled myself off the bed, made an attempt at straightening the blanket. "Come on in."

Mavis parted the beaded curtain and stepped aside as Charlie Rivers ducked his head and sidled into the room. He admired my sling. "Some people will do anything to get a little sympathy, won't they?"

"Is it working?"

"I doubt it. I couldn't find flowers, and if I brought candy, people would talk."

"If you don't need anything," Mavis said, "I'll see you tomorrow."

She disappeared through the beads, and Charlie looked around the apartment. "Nice. You've got enough room to meet yourself coming and going."

"How many of these wisecracks you got?"

He walked over to one of the movie shelves. "Have you watched all these?"

"Most of them."

"What are you going to do when you run out of room?"

"Buy more shelves." I gestured for him to sit in the easy chair.

"So you found an enemy, huh?"

"Or they found me. Any of your people been at the shooting scene?"

"Yeah. They didn't find any brass. Or anything else."

"There were some kids in a red pickup. You talk to them?"

"We did. They said there was a black SUV nearby. They didn't get a plate."

"Somebody was tailing me."

"Notice anyone?"

"No."

Charlie got up and tried to pace the cramped room. "We detained the Burgess kid yesterday."

"Really? I don't figure him for it."

"I'm not sure I do either, but there's some discrepancy in his story. He told us that after getting the Weddington prescription and putting it by her bed, he left the trailer to get something to eat."

"Right. He told me he was gone from nine to nine-thirty. The woman that runs the craft services table corroborated that. Julie somebody."

"Julie Travers. During our conversation with her, she said she never saw Burgess."

"So she lied to one of us. Why?"

"Good question. If she gave us the straight story, where was Burgess? We'll hold him for as long as we can. See if we can shake anything else out of him."

"Elaine seemed to like him. Where's his motive, Charlie?"

"Hell, I don't know. But he's the last person before Weddington to have handled that bottle. And his prints weren't on it. Just Weddington's."

"So you think he switched the bottles?"

"Maybe. But that raises another problem."

"What?"

"Where'd he get a bottle for the poison?"

I thought back to my conversation with Jody Burgess. "He told me it was the second time he'd picked up the prescription."

"So he could have filled an empty with poison."

"Or gotten a bottle from Goldberg. Sam gave me the impression his tooth had been bothering him for a while."

"We could read that to mean Burgess and Goldberg were accomplices."

"We could. If we could invent a motive for Burgess. I came across another angle. I talked to Janet Moreland again after Elaine's funeral. She told me she came to the lot earlier that morning."

"Earlier than when she was called?"

"Right. She said she had forgotten her script and came to pick it up."

"Why didn't she tell us that?"

"She told me that with all the turmoil after the body was discovered, it slipped her mind."

"You buy it?"

"They told me at the fitness place that they couldn't remember her being there. Did you check the place out?"

"We did. She logged in, so she must have been there. They've got a bar code on those membership cards and 'J. Moreland' logged in a little after nine."

"They have video cameras?"

"No. When does she say she came to pick up her script?"

"After her workout."

"So her story checks, as far as we know."

I felt vaguely disappointed. "Have you gotten anywhere on the Murphy killing?"

"Same problem. Same carnival midway. Nobody can place anybody anywhere."

"They're still shooting the picture?"

"Yeah. Filming around Weddington, I guess. Whatever that means. This Leslie Anderson has taken over for Murphy. If it was up to me, I would have cut my losses and shut the whole damn thing down. Doesn't look like Goldberg's gonna do that."

Chapter Thirty-Two

The guy next to me at the iHop finished his breakfast and left behind his *Los Angeles Times*. I snatched the paper because I had been reading a small, local-page story over his shoulder.

> Joey Hicks, 46, manager of the Cricket Lounge, was found dead in an alley behind the Sunset Strip nightclub. Police suspect he was robbed. An empty bank deposit pouch was found near the body.

Robbery? I wouldn't bet on it. At the same time, I wouldn't take even money that Hicks had called Sam Goldberg after our confrontation. Having given me Goldberg's name, Hicks would want to pretend we'd never met.

The investigations were stalled. I hadn't talked to Charlie Rivers in two days. Mavis and I hadn't tracked down the right Rodney Sullivan or Travis Wormstead. Shirley Jackson hadn't called.

I spent twenty minutes back at the office, then struggled into my coat.

"Where are you going," Mavis demanded. "Just in case I have to come and pick up the pieces."

"I'm going back to Americana and take up where I left off."

I sat in a line of vehicles at the front gate of Americana, second-guessing myself about having kept the phone list from Charlie Rivers. If my purpose was to protect Elaine's good name, I was being absurd. She was beyond caring what the media said about her. The police might have made headway with the list while I spun my wheels. They might have had Rodney Sullivan in the jug for days, and I might not be driving one-and-a-half-handed.

What I should do was dump everything I knew about Hodges, Pappas, Hicks Sullivan, and Goldberg right in Charlie's lap.

A UPS truck in front of me pulled up to the gate. The security guard, Jack Simmons, accompanied the driver to the rear of the truck and compared the manifest to the cartons. Security had gotten tighter at the studio.

The truck lumbered forward. I pulled my vehicle pass from where it was clipped to the visor. Jack Simmons pointed to the sling on my arm. "What happened to you?"

"Some asshole couldn't shoot straight."

"You return the favor?"

"Didn't get the chance."

He leaned into the window. "You haven't got anything in your trunk to blow up the place, do you?"

"Not today."

"Good. I'm off in a few minutes and I'm tired of looking at empty trunks." He pushed a button and the wooden gate lifted.

The big door of Stage 7 was open. I walked in, found Leslie Anderson finishing a conversation with a couple of grips. A headset spanned her straight blond hair. "What happened to you?" she said.

"Lover's quarrel. How goes the shoot?"

"It's a disaster. Dean Snider thinks so too. But Mr. Goldberg is determined to finish it."

"What are they doing with Elaine's scenes?"

"Shooting over a stand-in's shoulder. Long shots with a double. Apparently someone's going to dub her dialogue. I don't know if it's going to work."

I said, "I heard that you were made first AD. Congratulations."

"Thanks. I wish it had happened under different circumstances."

From behind we heard "watch your back" and stepped aside for a piece of scenery being pushed by two grips. I asked, "Is there going to be a funeral service for Betty?"

"No. Her family made arrangements for her to be sent back to Indiana."

I nodded. I asked for the day's call sheet, and she took me to a wheeled podium, pulled out a sheet and handed it to me.

Crew members are generally listed on the reverse side. I flipped it over to see if by chance the name Rodney Sullivan appeared anywhere. It didn't.

"You ever hear of a Rodney Sullivan," I asked. "Maybe floating around the production?"

She thought for a moment and shook her head. "Not that I remember."

I nodded. "I see Janet's on hold."

"Correct."

"Betty gave me her phone number and address. Can I get Madeline's from you?"

She consulted a list at the podium, scribbled a note. "Okay?"

"Great."

The queue at the gate inched forward. Jack Simmons was gone. He'd been replaced by a guard I didn't know, who spoke to a petite woman driving a big black SUV ahead of me. She had a couple of kids on board, maybe coming from an audition as hell children, who thought it was fun to make faces at me. The guard was being a stickler. He had the woman get out. She opened the rear door, got the kids out, and the guard lifted the rear seat and looked beneath it.

That was when it hit me.

And that's when I almost hit an incoming Mercedes as I made a sharp U-turn and squealed into the parking ramp.

Chapter Thirty-Three

The head of security for the Americana lot was Paul Thompson. He was tall, in his forties, and wore his uniform as if he were poured into it. I sat in front of his desk, watching him flip through pages of log entries the guards keep at the studio gate.

The security office was one of those mobile homes plopped down on permanent foundations. They're all over the lots in Hollywood. Despite looking rather Spartan from the outside, the interior was comfortable. Pots of coffee sat on burners next to a small sink. Several desks shared the oblong room. A large map of the Americana lot hung on one wall. In the far corner, two easy chairs flanked a sofa and a magazine-laden coffee table.

Sprawled on the sofa was Al Butler. He had been on guard duty the day Elaine died. Armando Rijos, another guard, sat across from Butler, his feet on the coffee table.

"Give me a minute here, Mr. Collins," Thompson said. His fingers rifled the pages of the log.

"No camera on the gate?"

"Are you kidding? What Goldberg lays out for security doesn't give him state-of-the-art records. I've been trying to coax him into getting this stuff computerized. He won't listen. Some of these logs look like they were written by chimpanzees." He turned to look at his two guards. Rijos flipped him the bird. Butler was not amused.

"Now, you're saying Janet Moreland came on the lot when?"

"I was told somewhere around ten that morning. Moreland said she had forgotten her script."

Thompson turned and looked at Rijos. "Armando, you saw her coming through?"

"Yeah, boss. I remember her, but I don't know the time exactly. I didn't log her in."

"Why not?"

"She was behind a Fedex truck. I had to look in the back of it. She was yelling at me. I told her to go around the truck and go through."

"Do you normally log in every vehicle?" I asked.

"We do," Thompson replied. "If the vehicle comes on for just the day, or a few hours, we give them a pass and collect it when they leave. People like Moreland who are on the lot for an extended period of time have a different colored pass. Sometimes we just wave them through without logging it in. Depends on how the traffic is. If Armando was busy and she was pissed, the smart thing would be to just wave her through."

"So there wouldn't be a record of her coming on the lot?"

"No, except for the guards seeing her." Thompson picked up his coffee cup, walked over to the sink. "All right. Armando, I'm not riding you here, but you're sure you remember the Moreland woman coming on the lot?"

Rijos took his feet off the coffee table and sat up on the edge of his chair. "Paul, I'm telling you, she came on the lot. I walked around to the back of the Fedex truck. She rolled down her window and yelled at me to hurry up. She said she had to pick up something. Then had to leave again. Could I hurry it up? I told her to go around the goddamn truck. She didn't even thank me. Just zipped up her window and squealed around the truck. Damn near hit somebody walking out of the parking ramp."

"Can you give me a ballpark time?" Thompson said.

"Look and see when there's a Fedex truck logged in. It'll be around then."

Thompson sat down behind his desk and said, "Well, help me out here. I can't read this damn handwriting."

Rijos got up from his chair and hopped over to Thompson's desk, imitating a chimp in transit. The antic cracked Butler up. Thompson rolled his eyes as Rijos grabbed the logbook and flipped a couple of pages. He pointed to one and handed the book to Thompson. "Right there. Fedex. Eight-forty."

Rijos walked back to his chair and Thompson looked at me. "Sounds like she's got her time mixed up."

"Would seem so, wouldn't it?"

Thompson turned back to Rijos. "What time did she leave?"

"I don't know," Rijos replied. "I was on the incoming side. Simmons was checking the outgoing."

Thompson nodded. "You guys know if Al has left for the day?"

Butler roused himself. "Yeah, I think he said he had to go buy some bananas."

Rijos let loose with a guffaw and held up his hand for Butler's high five.

Thompson muttered and picked up his phone. "Let me see if I can get Simmons on his cell."

I walked over to rinse my coffee cup.

I heard Thompson say, "Jack, this is Paul. I've got a Mr. Eddie Collins here in the office. I'm going to put you on the speaker phone."

Simmons's voice filled the office. "What's the matter now, Eddie? Somebody else shoot you?"

"Jack, I need to ask you about the day of the Weddington murder. Armando figures Janet Moreland drove on the lot a little before nine that morning. Do you remember that?"

"Yeah, she was honking behind some truck. Armando finally told her to go around."

"Do you remember when she came back through?"

"Well, let me see. It was ten, fifteen minutes later."

"You're sure?"

"Yeah."

"She had a two o'clock call that afternoon, Jack. I was told she came back around twelve-thirty. Do you recall that?"

"She did come back later. I'm not sure when. You should have it there. I remember logging her in."

Thompson referred to the logbook. "Here she is. Twelve-forty."

"We've got it, Jack," I said. "She and the Schmidt woman are down as coming back through at twelve-forty."

"Not both of them."

"What?"

"Moreland's friend, Madeline Schmidt? She wasn't in the car at twelve-forty."

"You're sure."

"Damn right. She's always riding me about how I should be taking acting lessons." We heard him laughing. "As if that's all I need, for God's sake. She wasn't in the car, Eddie."

I said, "Okay, Jack. Thanks a lot."

Thompson broke the connection.

I turned to Rijos. "Was Moreland alone at eight-forty?"

"With all the yelling she was doing, I made a point of looking at her. She was alone."

"Was she driving her Mercedes?"

"I don't remember if it was a Mercedes."

"But it wasn't an SUV?"

"No. That I'm sure of."

I got up, turned to Thompson. "You guys normally look into the trunk of every car coming on the lot?"

"As a rule," he said. "But between you and me and the gate post, if we have people coming on every day over a period of weeks, we don't generally bother."

"Thanks for your trouble, Paul. Appreciate it."

"No problem."

Chapter Thirty-Four

Ry Cooder kept me company as I crawled north along the 405 Freeway. Cooder was singing "Smack Dab in the Middle." The song aptly described Janet Moreland and Madeline Schmidt, smack dab in the middle of lies.

I'd thought I'd had an inspiration, waiting in the security line, on how someone like Rodney Sullivan might have gotten on the lot, smuggled in by a driver unknown. Right away the guards' information had pointed elsewhere. Both men who had let Janet Moreland enter insisted she had been alone. Neither had checked the trunk—or probably even the floor in the back seat—of her car. Leslie Anderson had seen Moreland and Madeline Schmidt unloading groceries in the early afternoon. Schmidt said she didn't drive. So how had she gotten on the lot to help Moreland with those Whole Foods bags? I kicked myself. I should have asked the security crew if Schmidt had arrived by taxi or with another driver.

As for Moreland, why had she insisted she had picked up the script *after* the workout? Why, except to establish that she hadn't been on the lot before 9 a.m.

Had she even been at the 24 Hour Fitness Club that morning? Her membership card had been scanned, but who had presented it? The "J. Moreland" on the sign-in log was gender neutral. With no video surveillance cameras, anyone could have had the card.

I got off the 405 and onto Sunset, which yellow plastic cones narrowed to one lane as I passed the entrance to Will Rogers State Park. Rocks and gravel had fallen on the road from the recent rains. Looking for my turn, I slowed and headlights appeared in my mirror and stayed close. The cones ended and I pulled into the right hand lane to let him pass. He didn't. I gripped the steering wheel in apprehension. Was the driver Sullivan? Had he followed me from Americana? Then the vehicle swung out and blasted past, a honk and a lifted middle finger bidding me goodbye.

I relaxed and found Via de La Paz. It was a stately neighborhood, and the Reese-Moreland digs didn't shame it. A Mercedes sat in the driveway next to a black SUV.

I drove past. A man and a tow-headed boy were tossing a football in the front yard. I parked a few doors down and walked back.

The house was long and one-storied, painted off-white. Flowerbeds ran its length. Large picture windows flanked the front door. A sidewalk bisected a neatly trimmed lawn. A bicycle lay on its side by the front stoop. A spiked iron fence kept me out. Both the driveway gate and a smaller pedestrian gate had mounted keypads.

The football tossing had stopped. The man came down to the sidewalk. He was easy to recognize, short and a little paunchy with a neatly clipped moustache and goatee.

"Can I help you?" he said.

I held my license against two iron bars. "I'm involved in the investigation of Elaine Weddington's murder. I wonder if I could speak to your wife."

"Janet has already talked to the police."

"I know. She's also talked to me. There are new developments. This won't take long."

We went inside and Reese gestured to a living room on the left. "Why don't you wait in there. I'll tell Janet you're here." He picked up a pamphlet from a small table in the foyer. "Something for you to look at."

As he disappeared down the hallway, I glanced at the pamphlet. It was a pitch for his political campaign. I slipped it into my coat pocket and looked around. Across the hall was a formal dining room with a table big enough for the tow-headed kid's whole football team. Above a sideboard hung a print of the praying hands by Albrecht Durer. A reminder to say grace before meals, I supposed.

There was some of the same in the living room, above a gas fireplace a picture of the Christ kneeling in prayer. It left no doubt as to what this family did on Sundays. Behind one of the three sofas stood a glass-topped table supporting a crystal obelisk. I went over and had a look. The engraving on the crystal celebrated Janet Moreland's performance in a picture I vaguely remembered seeing.

"Good afternoon, Mr. Collins."

I turned to find Janet standing in the entrance to the living room. She was dressed in jeans, a turtleneck and running shoes. I nodded to the obelisk.

"Congratulations."

"Thank you. It was a wonderful part. I was very fortunate. Have a seat. How were you able to find me?"

"The studio gave me your address."

She arched her eyebrows and nodded. "I see." She sat across from me. An ornate coffee table separated us. Precisely on the table's center was a Bible. I was beginning to feel a little pressured. Well, what can I do for you, Mr. Collins? I hear they've arrested Jody Burgess. Surely your investigation should be over?"

"He hasn't been charged yet. The case remains open."

"I see. How can I help?"

"Straight answers would help."

"I've given you straight answers, but I'm happy to give you more. What about?"

"The day of Elaine's murder."

"Haven't I been over this? Both with you and the police."

"Yes, ma'am. But there's still a couple of things I'm not clear on."

"And what would those be?"

"How did Madeline Schmidt get to the studio that day?"

"I beg your pardon?"

"The guards at the gate tell me that when you drove onto the lot at twelve-forty, Madeline wasn't with you."

"You're right. She wasn't."

"Even though you had just been studying with her?"

"I had some errands to run after she and I were through. She said she would catch a cab to the studio."

"But she was there to help you unload your car?" I didn't need to consult my notebook, but I looked at a couple of pages for show. "Bags from Whole Foods Market, I believe."

"Yes, that was one of the errands. And yes, she was there to help me."

"So she arrived at the lot before you?"

"Obviously."

"Do you know what time she got there?"

"No, I'm afraid not. You're going to have to ask her."

"I'll do that," I said. "She lives in the Los Feliz area, I believe. That's a pretty good cab ride, isn't it?"

She uttered a soft laugh and ran one hand over the back of the sofa. "When was the last time you took a cab in L.A., Mr. Collins?"

"Been some time."

"For me as well. If I remember correctly, cab drivers seem to pay little heed to speed limits."

I grinned. "You told me that you were at your workout from approximately eight to nine that morning."

"Yes."

"The gate guards at Americana have you coming in at roughly eighty-forty?" For a fleeting moment, I thought I'd delivered one from left field.

"I'm sure I don't know, Mr. Collins. They're obviously mistaken."

"They tell me you were behind a Fedex truck that was logged onto the lot at eight-forty. You were laying on your horn. They said you were finally told to go around the truck. The other guard says you came back through about ten or fifteen minutes later."

"I was indeed behind a truck. I couldn't tell you if it was Fedex. And I wouldn't characterize myself as 'laying' on my horn. I was impatient, and for very good reason."

"Because you were running late?"

"I was running behind, but that wasn't what was making me impatient. The guard and the driver were standing at the rear of the truck having some sort of private moment between them, laughing and what have you. Very inconsiderate. The guard seemed to have no interest in looking inside the truck. Anyway, when I finally did get his attention, he told me to go around. But it wasn't eight-forty. Nine-twenty, nine-thirty would be more accurate."

"They've got the time down on paper."

She shook her head and leaned forward. "With all due respect, I wouldn't put a great deal of validity in what those guards say."

"Why is that?"

"Several times I've tried to drive through that gate, and even with a drive-on pass, they don't know who I am. I would be skeptical of what they say."

"They've been there a long time."

"I'm sure they have. And therein could lie the problem. Perhaps Sam Goldberg should hire some new guards. Ones that don't remember Gable and Bogie. I was at 24 Hour Fitness at that time, and I believe they've confirmed that to the police."

We were interrupted by the squeal of a child. A little girl rounded the corner into the living room. She was blond and curly-haired. Blue eyes punctuated a round cherubic face. She bounded into the room and up to Janet.

"Mommy, Mommy, you gotta come right now."

Moreland took the little girl into her arms. "What's the matter, baby?"

"Anthony's being naughty."

"He is? What's he doing?" She glanced at the doorway.

Hal Reese had followed the girl. "Sorry, honey," Reese said. "The two of them are driving Inez crazy. Will you be long?"

The cherub turned to look at me and her lower lip protruded. I knew the domestic disturbance had been choreographed. The little girl was proud of having gotten her lines right.

"I'll be right there," Janet Moreland said. "Stephanie, go back in the kitchen, and—"

"Now, Mommy!"

"Yes, honey, right away."

She turned Stephanie around and pointed her toward her daddy.

"Nice meeting you, Mr. Collins," Reese said. "I hope I can count on your vote."

His wife stood. "I'm afraid I've got a bit of a family crisis back there. And we have campaign staff coming for dinner. I do hope you will excuse me."

"Of course."

"I'm glad to see your eye is healing. And I hope you're coping with Elaine's death. My prayers have been with you. We all mourn her loss."

Chapter Thirty-Five

I don't claim to know exactly what makes a good actor. If the eyes are windows to the soul, the answer has to be the sheer honesty that's projected through those windows by a good, solid professional.

Janet Moreland didn't make the cut. Having looked into her eyes several times, I didn't believe her for a minute. Granted a guard could make mistakes, but I would believe the guys at Americana long before I would believe Moreland.

Had she smuggled Madeline Schmidt onto the lot?

It seemed absurd, but evidence said she had.

Then why—to poison my ex-wife?

I didn't know how much I would get out of Madeline. By now Moreland would have phoned her. She either would have her story straight or would be in a cab heading for cover.

At the corner of Via de La Paz and Sunset, I waited for a break in east-bound traffic so I could make a right turn. Headlights hurtled through the afternoon fog. The car's heater was ten degrees behind the weather, and I was sore and cold. A car slid up next to me on my left. I looked at the driver.

Janet Moreland was behind the wheel.

She was edging her car forward, waiting to make a left turn. What happened to the campaign staff coming for dinner? A gap in traffic opened and she floored the car, heading toward the Pacific Coast Highway. It took me a little longer, but I laid down a little rubber as I crossed eastbound traffic and barreled west. Only one horn blared.

She hadn't gotten too far in front of me.

I was going to feel foolish if Moreland was popping out for something to feed the campaign staffers. But she glided through the main shopping area of Pacific Palisades, passed a Ralph's grocery, and continued toward the Pacific Coast Highway.

She was taking the curves at a good clip. The fog thinned as we approached the coast. The sun eerily glowed behind cloudbank offshore, like a forest fire threatening a distant ridge.

Janet's Mercedes approached the intersection of Sunset and the Pacific Coast Highway. She sidled into the right lane and flicked on her turn signal. She had no reason to know my car, so I stayed pretty close. The light changed and she headed north. She moved over to the left lane and sped up. The afternoon had started to fade, and surfers were hoisting boards onto the roofs of cars parked along the southbound shoulder.

The PCH is the major artery from the west side of L.A. up into Malibu, the stomping grounds of many of the Hollywood elite. I didn't think Janet Moreland belonged to that club.

I kept an eye on the mirror, but nothing behind me looked like a tail. I glanced down at the odometer. We had gone about three miles up the coast.

We passed Topanga Canyon Boulevard on the right. If Moreland was planning a circuitous route back to Madeline's place in Los Feliz, she had missed her turn. On the left, the ocean was losing the vestiges of daylight. Janet had settled into a steady pace of fifty-five. I kept her in sight from about a hundred yards behind.

I cracked my car window and enjoyed the smell of the sea air. Signs zipped by denoting Big Rock Beach, Las Flores Beach, La Costa Beach, Carbon Beach. We'd gone seven miles. The Malibu Pier appeared and just as quickly receded. We slowed and went through Malibu Colony Plaza.

At nine miles, the entrance to Pepperdine University loomed on the right. Still no headlights dogging me.

Dan Blocker Beach appeared on the left. Before I could get my mind working on how Hoss Cartwright got a strip of sand named after him, the Mercedes slowed into a left-turn lane.

A sign announced Cliffside Court. Under a single light pole was a guard shack. Wisps of fog clung to the light. About fifty yards north of the shack, a neon sign pointed out the Sand Castle Restaurant.

As I approached the stop sign, Janet made a U-turn, doubled back, and turned in at Cliffside Court.

A couple of oncoming vehicles passed before I could cross over the highway into the parking lot of the Sand Castle. I nosed the car up to a wooden, waist-high fence at the south boundary of the restaurant's parking lot. Rising up on my right was the sheer wall of a ridge that loomed between me and the ocean. It was maybe a hundred feet high. Sheets of plastic suspended from the top prevented erosion. The base of the ridge was lined with brush.

After a brief stop at the guard shack, Janet's Mercedes continued along a path to the top of the ridge. I didn't know what was up there. My first problem was to get by the guard in the shack. I reached up and switched off the car's dome light. I got out and squatted behind the fence. It took ten minutes before I had a break. Behind me, a couple came out of the restaurant, loud and happy, and got in their car. They drove as far as the gate to Cliffside Court, stopped and got the guard busy giving complicated directions.

I climbed over the fence and crept along the base of the ridge to the driveway. Behind me, the woman in the car was laughing. I headed uphill.

Chapter Thirty-Six

The layout at the top was nothing more than a glorified trailer court. A cluster of mailboxes at the entrance indicated eight addresses. The names Moreland or Reese didn't appear on any of them.

Four trailers were on either side of a center drive, separated by redwood fences. I started down the drive. The place had the trappings of a poor man's Malibu. Luxury autos nestled under carports. Satellite dishes perched on roofs. One trailer had a patio out front, complete with grill and picnic table. A small white picket fence surrounded its foundation.

I passed by the second trailer on the ocean side. The only sound I heard was the surf. It crashed against rocks, and in the fog-shrouded evening the sound was soothing.

Then the dog started barking.

A small white bundle of hair pranced over from the other side of the driveway, stopped a few feet in front of me and bounced on all four legs. Each bounce was punctuated by a bark. A door to one of the trailers opened. An elderly woman stuck her head out and yelled, "Lulu, be quiet. Come here."

Lulu didn't cooperate, forcing her owner to come out of the trailer to fetch her. As the woman opened her gate, a security light came on. She scurried over to me and picked up the yapper. "I'm sorry, Mr. Hines, I didn't—" She stopped when she straightened and saw my face. "Well, you're not Mr. Hines. Who are you, young man?"

"His brother Eddie, ma'am. Visiting for a couple of days. I was just getting some air."

"I see. Well, nice to meet you, Eddie. I'm Mrs. Merton. I guess you've already met Lulu here. I'm sorry she disturbed you. She's perfectly harmless."

"I'm sure she is, ma'am." I stretched out a hand to pet the little creature. My effort at conciliation was greeted by a menacing growl.

"Bad girl. Bad, bad girl." Mrs. Merton gave Lulu a little spank on the nose. "I'd better get her indoors." As she reached her doorway, she turned to get another glimpse of Mr. Hines's brother and I gave her a little wave.

I continued past the third trailer. Lulu's guard dog duties hadn't brought out anyone else.

The end of the driveway came into view. Across it ran a chain-link fence that stretched the width of the ridge. Through the fence I could see a vacant lot overgrown with brush.

At the last trailer on the left I saw the Mercedes. Redwood fencing made up the back wall of a carport. A wooden gate led to the front door. Both rear and front doors had small lights above them that barely penetrated the fog. A flagstone patio supported several potted plants.

Voices drifted from the trailer. I moved closer, skirting a platform that had been built to camouflage the trailer hitch. I wasn't silent. Pieces of a croquet set made the ground treacherous. The voices in the trailer stopped. I held my breath. They got going again, and I reached a window. Janet Moreland was sitting at a kitchen table across from Madeline Schmidt. A tote bag lay on the table near Moreland. Schmidt had her glasses off and dabbed at her eyes with tissue.

"Maddie, will you listen to me? I didn't tell him anything."

"Then how did he know you came on the lot early?"

"He talked to the gate guards. I said they were mistaken, but I don't think he believed me."

"Janet, listen to yourself. These lies aren't going to work anymore. Jody Burgess has been arrested. Do you think he's going to put himself in jeopardy? He's going to tell the police he had your fitness card."

"That doesn't mean they can put you in Elaine's trailer. I told Collins you took a cab to the studio."

"They'll check with the cab companies. When they don't find a record of it, they're going to force me to tell them." Madeline let go of more sobs. "Good God, stuck in the trunk of that car like some goddamn illegal immigrant or something. I can't do this anymore, Janet. I feel like I'm—" She broke off and started crying. I could hear the sounds of Janet trying to soothe her.

I peered through the window again when I heard Madeline's voice.

"No more lies, Janet. I want to stop."

"I'm not going to let some detective destroy what Hal and I have built. We've worked too hard. I don't let anyone take things away from me!" Her voice changed. "Maddie, Maddie, it's going to be all right. I called him before I left home. He said he'd take care of it. He's going to meet us here."

I had no idea who this "he" was, but I looked behind myself and wished I had brought a gun.

"What can he do, Janet? The police are—"

"Shhh. I think I heard something. It's probably him now. Get the door."

Janet pointed, and Madeline rose to open the front door. Janet stuck her hand inside the tote bag and pulled out a black adjustable wrench. When Madeline reached the door, Janet was a step behind her. She swung the wrench against the side of the woman's head.

Madeline started to fall, and Janet caught her. Holding the limp figure against the door with one hand, she tossed the wrench onto the table. Then she lifted Madeline into a fireman's carry. She crossed the room and opened the back door.

Chapter Thirty-Seven

I ran to intercept her. There was a small lawn behind the trailer, then a low stone retaining wall at the cliff's edge. On my third step, a croquet wicket snagged my foot and I landed hard. I got to my knees and yelled into the fog:

"Put her down, Janet!"

Moreland froze. When she recognized me, she whirled and rushed toward the wall. Beyond it was emptiness, straight down to the rocky shore. I reached her as she lowered Madeline onto the wall. I grabbed an arm and flung Moreland back across the lawn. Madeline started to slide. I lunged and pulled her back.

From behind I heard footsteps. I turned to see Janet charging me with a croquet mallet clenched in her fists. She wound up and swung. I barely had time to lift my right arm and take the force of the mallet below the elbow. I screamed as pain shot up my arm.

She came around with a back swing that caught me between the shoulder blades. I twisted as I fell and landed face-up. She straddled me, grimacing in fury, teeth clenched in determination, and swung the mallet overhand. This one would spatter my brains around. I rolled hard against her left boot, knocking her off balance, and the wooden head buried itself in the ground.

As Moreland fell, I twisted the mallet from her grip. I pushed her off me, got to my feet. I tossed the mallet seaward, then pulled Madeline Schmidt off the wall, onto the wet grass. I couldn't tell if she was breathing.

I heard a roar. Janet was coming again. This time she brandished one of the sharpened croquet stakes. She was a tough, strong woman in good shape from her workouts. Enough was enough. I brushed the stake aside and punched her in the nose. She sat down.

Madeline was groaning. I helped her sit up and leaned her against the wall.

She looked at me in surprise. "Collins! How did you—?"

"Moreland led me here."

"She *hit* me!" the woman complained.

"She also tried to throw you off the cliff."

"What?" She struggled to get to her feet.

"Stay down. You're hurt."

"Janet, is that true?"

There was no response.

"Are you telling me the truth?"

I nodded.

Fear and confusion filled her eyes. She buried her face in her hands. "Oh, my God! After all this, and she tries to kill me?" She started sobbing again, deep, agonizing gasps.

"Madeline, listen to me. Did you switch Elaine's medicine?"

"Maddie, don't tell him anything!" Janet Moreland screamed. She had risen to her knees.

"It's no use, Madeline," I said. "I overheard the conversation. You broke into Elaine's trailer and switched the bottles."

"Maddie, please don't." Janet began to creep toward us, shaking her head from side to side.

"It's over, Madeline," I said. "Tell me. You switched the bottles."

After a long moment, she stopped sobbing and said, "Yes."

There it was. Simple. Precise.

I looked out into the darkness over the ocean, listening to the surf. "Did you kill Betty Murphy too?"

"No, *she* did."

Once again, simple and precise.

Janet gave a low, wrenching sob. She came up to Madeline. Her hair was disheveled. She looked helpless. Blood ran from her nose. I could sense the desperation in her. She clutched her head, almost as if she were trying to blot out the finality of the confession. She grabbed her friend by the wrists. "No, no, Maddie, please don't."

"Don't touch me! I don't want you near me."

"I'm sorry! I panicked. I'll make it up to you."

"No. No more lies, no more secrets." The woman jerked her wrists away, and Janet Moreland stumbled backward.

Her heels hit the retaining wall. Her arms flailed. I lurched toward her, but it was like trying to move in the deep end of a swimming pool. The sequence had the look of a slow-motion scene, where the director attempts to freeze time.

She went backwards, frame by frame. Arms churning as she tried to regain her balance. Then screaming. Then gone.

Madeline shrieked and leapt for the edge. She had a leg over the wall when I caught her and wrestled her back onto the wet grass.

"Let me go, let me go!"

"Too late, Madeline. It's too late."

She broke down and fell to her knees, sobbing uncontrollably. I put an arm across her shoulders.

The voice came out of the fog from behind me.

"Well, now, ain't this a touching scene?"

Sam Goldberg stepped out of the fog. He had a gun pointed at me.

Chapter Thirty-Eight

Madeline's fingers dug into my thigh. "Janet did call him."

"Yeah, she called me," Sam said, "She said the two of you were having a little get-together out here." He waved the barrel of the gun to his left. "Didn't expect you, though, m'boy. Get up and move away from her."

I stood and edged to my left.

"Too bad I missed Janet," Sam said. "But it's probably better. Two broads falling off a cliff after a lover's quarrel. Tragic." He gave a guttural laugh. "They tell you about themselves, Eddie?"

I didn't answer.

He turned to Madeline. "What's a matter, honey? You get coy and shy all of a sudden?" He let out another guffaw. "They weren't being shy when I caught 'em in the sack."

Madeline scrambled to her feet. "Shut your mouth, you filthy asshole." She turned to me. "He's the one responsible for Elaine's death. He blackmailed Janet into doing it."

I looked at Sam, this man I'd known for years, almost a mentor. A man to whom Elaine had been loyal. "Sam?"

"You don't wanna know, m'boy." He grinned. "And even if you do, I'm not going to tell you."

Madeline Schmidt had her arms wrapped around herself. I asked, "Why?"

"Sam—Sam threatened to make it public. To tell Janet's husband about us."

"So what? Being gay in Hollywood is no big deal, Madeline."

"It is if you're Janet Moreland and you're married to Hal Reese."

"She's right, Eddie," said Sam. "Evangelical Councilman Reese? Mr. Family Values running for mayor? So squeaky-clean his wife can't get laid so she has to shack up with another woman. You could kiss that campaign goodbye."

"Janet would sooner have died," Madeline said.

Sam shifted the gun to his left hand and moved toward Madeline. He grabbed her arm, pushed her toward the wall. "Time to join your sweetheart," he said. She struggled, and he cracked the gun barrel on the back of her head. She sank to her knees.

As he bent to pick her up, I lifted the croquet stake from the grass.

There was a high-pitched bark from a dog, and Mrs. Merton stuck her head through the gate.

"Miss Moreland, are you all right? I heard someone screaming."

Sam turned in her direction. As the gun came up, I swung the stake down and smashed his wrist. He screamed in pain. The gun went off and fell to the lawn. I jammed the blunt end of the stake into his belly. While he was gasping, I picked up the gun.

Mrs. Merton tried to make herself heard over the shrill barking. "Mr. Hines, what is—?"

I called to her, "I want you to go back to your trailer and call nine-one-one. A woman has been killed. Tell them to send an ambulance. Maybe two."

"Killed? Who's been—?"

"Just do it. Can you do that for me, Mrs. Merton?"

"Yes, yes, of course." She scurried off.

Sam was trying to pull himself off the ground.

"Stay down. Just stay the fuck on the ground!" I kept the gun on him. He rolled onto his back, coughing and wheezing. "Why did you do it, Sam?"

He peered up at me, venom in his eyes. "Fuck you."

I aimed the gun to the right of his head and fired a round into the lawn.

"God damn you, you crazy bastard!"

"Tell me about Joey Hicks. Did you kill him too?"

"I don't know any Joey Hicks."

I aimed to the left of his head and fired. He yelped, then dug his heels into the grass and tried to push himself away from me, like a big beached crab. I stepped on one of his ankles. "Hicks told me you were running a call girl ring. A guy named Milt Pappas called it 'Sleep With a Star.' Elaine was part of it, wasn't she?"

"I don't know what the fuck you're talking about."

I dropped one knee into the middle of his chest and stuck the barrel of the gun into his right eye socket.

"Was Elaine part of it?"

He winced and scrunched his other eye shut. "Yes, goddammit."

"Why did you do it?"

"She owed me."

"Owed you what?"

"Money. I gave her money."

"For what?"

"You don't wanna know."

I glared down at him. Rage welled inside me. I cracked his forehead with the gun and fired another round into the lawn.

"Listen, you sleazy son of a bitch. This was not the Elaine Weddington I knew. Why did you give her money, Sam?" He didn't answer me. I pulled back the hammer of the gun and stuck it back in his eye socket.

"Okay, okay! You're fucking nuts!" He started coughing, sounding like he was choking.

"Why did she want the money?"

"She had a kid. She wasn't making the bucks yet. I gave her the money to take care of it."

I froze, my finger on the trigger, not sure I had heard him correctly.

"Is this some kind of sick joke?"

"It's no goddamn joke. She had a baby girl. Her career was taking off and she didn't want to raise it. She put it out for adoption. I gave her enough money for a trust fund."

"And in return you put her in a call girl ring?"

"It wasn't a call girl ring. It was higher class than that. We helped each other, some of the actresses and me. I don't have any fucking conglomerates backing my pictures. I raise my own goddamn money. Now and then I have to repay a favor or two."

"With sex."

"Sex, a trip to Vegas. Hawaii. A picture in the paper with a star. What the hell's the difference?" He tried to prop himself on an elbow. "These girls don't make a million bucks a picture. They can use a little extra."

"And Elaine?"

"She wanted more. A piece of my studio. She threatened to go to the cops."

I pulled the gun away from his eye and stared down at him. I wanted to kill him right there. The story would be easy enough to concoct for the police. No witnesses. We had struggled for the gun. Five shots went off. The fifth one got him in the chest.

"Who's the father, Sam?"

"She didn't say."

"Answer the goddamn question! Who was the father?"

Tears started to fall from his eyes. "It was you, you fuckin' loser."

He literally spat the words at me. His breath reeked of stale cigar. I looked at his red face, streaked with tears and blood. After a moment, I took my knee off his chest and stood up. He rolled over on his side, struggling for breath.

"When Elaine kicked your ass out, she was pregnant. She didn't want you to know."

"Why not?"

"How should I know? You should have asked her." He pulled a handkerchief from his pocket and wiped the blood off his forehead. "Maybe she didn't want a drunk raising her kid."

"Where's the girl?"

"Leave her alone, Eddie."

"I want to know where she lives, Sam. You at least owe me that."

"I don't owe you shit. Cincinnati. Her name is Kelly. Kelly Robinson. Her adopted father is a teacher. Her mother runs a real estate office." He sat up and looked at me. "Now leave me the fuck alone."

I watched him as he rolled over to his knees and continued coughing. From behind I heard faint moans from Madeline.

And off in the distance the wail of a siren.

Chapter Thirty-Nine

When the police came, Madeline wouldn't shut up. She had switched the medicine bottles in Elaine's trailer. She had stood watch while Janet entered the production trailer and strangled Betty Murphy. That had had to happen because Betty tipped her hand about having seen Janet on the lot the previous morning. The women had followed me to Milt Pappas's place, and on to Hicks's joint, and when she had the chance Moreland had shot me. Charlie Rivers arrived in time to hear most of it. After a while, I went outside. When they brought Madeline Schmidt out in handcuffs, she said softly, "I'm very sorry, Mr. Collins."

I gave an LASD lieutenant the name and address of Janet Moreland's husband. He said, "That the City Councilman? The one running for mayor?"

"That's him."

"Any kids?"

"Boy and a girl."

"Oh, crap."

We passed the Cliffside Court mailboxes on the way to Charlie's car. He tapped one of the boxes. "Moreland and Schmidt rented this hideaway in the name of Tony Step Productions. Mean anything to you?"

"No."

"Schmidt says it was for Anthony and Stephanie, Moreland's children. Nice, huh?"

"Is Goldberg talking?"

"Not even to bluff. He's waiting for his lawyer. What Schmidt says about the blackmail, I don't know about that. You blackmail someone for money. But to commit a murder? Schmidt says we don't understand. Moreland was going to be the mayor's wife. And besides, Moreland and your ex were rivals, bitching about who would get top billing in that dumb movie. So Goldberg had to push, but not that hard. Maybe I'll believe it if I hear him say it."

"He's a believable guy," I said.

"I'll give you a shout if I need anything else for my report. The DA'll probably call you to testify."

"Yeah, I figured that."

I drove home, not minding the fog. A lot of things looked better in it.

I tried wrapping my head around was the fact that I was a father. The term seemed incompatible with me. Somewhere in Cincinnati was a girl born to a mother who didn't want to raise her and a father who knew nothing of her existence.

As the lights of Santa Monica loomed on my left, I began to wonder about Kelly Robinson. Who did she look like? Was she happy? Would I ever have the opportunity to see her?

The questions stayed with me as I headed east on the Santa Monica Freeway. The fog had dissipated, but the questions stayed.

Epilogue

Elaine always liked jonquils, so I took a bunch with me. The lady at the flower shop had been a talker. Jonquils are really daffodils, which come from the family Narcissus. In Greek mythology, Narcissus fell in love with his own image and turned into the flower. The story would have been perfect if he'd been the first actor.

Vince Ferraro had sent me an email with a photograph he'd found in Elaine's study. Kelly was a very pretty little girl. Dark hair hung to her shoulders, arranged in ringlets. Her eyes were brown and looked like they were brimming with glee at having her picture taken. Her cheeks were rosy and complemented with dimples.

The picture lay next to the jonquils in the front seat of my car. I turned off Barham into the entrance of Forest Lawn Hollywood Hills. Cars dotted the curbs of the paved streets. Sadness was filling someone's day.

A headstone had been placed at the grave. The small piece of granite had a metal plate inlaid that listed her name and the years of her birth and her death. I leaned the arrangement of jonquils against the headstone.

I wasn't certain what had drawn me here after the events of the last weeks. A need to have one last talk with her? It was a conversation we probably should have had years ago. I squatted on my haunches and held Kelly's snapshot in front of me.

Vince sent me this picture, Elaine. I think she looks more like you than me. A smile as big as the sky. I wish you had told me she was coming. But I guess by then we had run out of things to say. I didn't know the words, Elaine, or even how to say them if I had known. An actor in need of a script . . . I didn't know how to love you. Maybe I didn't want to. But I'm glad we shared what we did. And I'm glad for Kelly. . . .

I stood and gazed down at this finality of a life lived. A slight breeze toppled the flower arrangement and I righted it. From here I could see the sound stages of Warner Brothers and Disney, and I felt suddenly heartened by the thought that Elaine's image was forever preserved on film. Maybe someday Kelly would learn who that woman was.

I lowered myself behind the steering wheel of my car, slid the window down and raised my face to the afternoon sun. It felt good.

About the Author

Clive Rosengren has spent the better part of the last 40 years as an actor, 18 of them pounding the same streets as Eddie Collins in *Murder Unscripted*. Numerous TV and film credits include playing the only character to have thrown Sam Malone out of *Cheers*. He lives in Ashland, Oregon, where he's working on a second Eddie Collins novel.

Hollywood & *Crime*

"Faherty writes this era like he was there." *Crime Spree*

A brand new story plus classics from the two-time Shamus winner.

THE HOLLYWOOD OP Terence Faherty
246 pages $14.95
ISBN: 978-1-935797-08-1

In Hollywood *and* Washington, a good secret is worth your life. A movie is about to expose a war-hero President, and PI—and ex-con—Hayes is targeted for the cutting-room floor.

LONG PIG James L. Ross
318 pages $15.95
ISBN: 978-1-935797-10-4

Booklist Starred Review
"Fans of detective fiction will love this novel!"

A film turns Galileo's life into a bawdy farce, and the credited scriptwriter is dead. Chess Hanrahan probes more than one kind of murder.

HONORS DUE Edward Cline
168 pages $14.95
ISBN: 978-1-935797-14-2

CPSIA information can be obtained at www.ICGtesting.com
Printed in the USA
LVOW091507130612

285980LV00010B/69/P